A WALK IN THE SUN

LISA DOMINIQUE MACHAT

Set in the late 1800s in both England and France, A Walk in the Sun is a passionate tale of love, anguish, guilt, and revenge told through the eyes of Nicholas Justine. Nicholas, a lonely mortal born into wealth yet neglected from birth, is transformed into a naïve young vampire. Desperately trying to deal with his sudden immortal curse, he clings onto his hopes of marrying his Elena, a beautiful and compassionate mortal.

Their love becomes an unbreakable bond as Nicholas struggles to comprehend his new-found powers and curse. Only a force greater than himself could threaten his life and the woman he adores. Be it fate or the devil, a challenge is unleashed when suddenly Elena and Nicholas come face to face with the ruthless and cunning Count Victor Du Fay. A master of the occult, Du Fay is a follower of the left-hand path, a black magician driven by greed and the power to prevail. His attraction to Elena leads the vampire and the devil's chosen disciple to a duel like no other.

Will Du Fay destroy Nicholas? Will Elena's love overpower evil? Full of plot twists and turns, this story takes you on an emotional journey that will capture your heart and awaken your soul. Through joy and sorrow, passion and hate, and bittersweet enchantment, this vampire thriller will keep you turning pages to find out more.

A WALK
IN THE
SUN

~

A VAMPIRE NOVEL

BY

LISA DOMINIQUE MACHAT

This book is dedicated to my son Nicholas,
who is my hope, love, and joy in life.

Prologue

I have tasted the treasures of life's kiss
Watched lovers stroll lonely footpaths
With secrets untold.
I have ignited passion to dreams
Lifted lost faces out of their darkness.
If you look into my eyes,
You may see visions of my past
Where I was born
How and why I became what I am.
I am Nicholas Justine.
I am a vampire,
And this is my story.

Chapter One

My Mortal Beginnings

*T*he year was 1874, and the snow lay heavily on the grounds of Justine Manor. My mother's cries echoed down the corridor of the west side of the house as the doctor struggled to deliver her first child. She had known Dr. Reims all her life. My mother looked up into his eyes and grasped his hand like a desperate child.

"Timothy, is everything all right?"

"Yes, Emily." He smiled reassuringly, and wiped the perspiration from her forehead. Everything is fine."

Dr. Reims asked my mother to bear down once more as she carried on into her eighteenth hour of labor. Meanwhile, my father waited downstairs in his study, nervous and anxious. Trying not to worry, he paced the floor and watched the clock. He had never felt so useless, so vulnerable, so scared. Standing at his desk, he finished another glass of port.

"How much longer?" he asked. "What is the doctor doing?"

My father was a man of little patience. Used to being in control, he refused to tolerate fools. He was recognized in High Society as being one of the best solicitors in London, becoming powerful and successful, respected and feared. He was a solicitor who had never lost a case, a man obsessed with winning the game. There was only one person he didn't judge or try to control and that was my mother, for he adored everything about her. He loved her beyond words. Emily was his world. He couldn't bear to hear her crying out in pain.

"Goddammit," he said. "It has been eighteen hours, how much longer does she have to suffer?"

As the clock struck 7:04 a.m., my mother bore down one last time. A gasp of joy filled her room as Dr. Reim announced she had given birth to a boy. Suddenly that joy turned into panic, as he saw my mother begin to tremble. Something was wrong. My mother was bleeding heavily and had lost consciousness. Quickly, Dr. Reim tried to stop the bleeding, but there was nothing he could do to stem her hemorrhaging. For the next thirty minutes, he fought to save her until the room fell in silence, and my mother lay lifeless.

Charlotte, my nanny, held me in her arms, comforting my cries as the two nurses began to prepare the room for my father to enter. Clean blankets were arranged over my mother from her shoulders to her feet. The basket of bloody sheets and towels had been covered over near the dresser. Dr. Reim sat devastated, too upset to speak.

Thank God the baby had survived, he thought. But why, God? Why did Emily have to die? Pulling himself up, he left the room and made his way down the stairs to my father's study. It was said that when my father heard the news, he rushed up the stairs. Not willing to accept that nothing could save my mother, he tried to wake her. Holding her in his arms, sobbing uncontrollably, he begged her to come back. Kissing her pale lifeless face, he cried out her name, lost in disbelief.

"Emily, Emily, I can't live without you," he wept. "Please don't leave me, please don't leave me." As Charlotte carried me out of the room, my father never asked to see his newborn son. That was the day he lost his world, the day he decided to push me aside. As the winter sun shone through the window and kissed my mother's face goodbye, an empty silence came over Justine Manor.

My mother was laid to rest only one mile from the house in the village churchyard in Essex, and it seemed as the snow fell and laid its blanket upon the many wreaths and flowers at her graveside, the heart of Justine manner had laid itself to rest beside her.

I was named Nicholas Edward Justine, a name my mother had chosen for me. My room faced the north side of the house. It had two large windows where I could look down onto the courtyard and servants' quarters.

My nanny, Charlotte, raised me with much love and care. As the seasons changed and the years passed by, she had requested many times that I might be moved to a brighter room with a view of the trees and extensive grounds. But my father insisted that the room I had slept in since birth was satisfactory.

My years growing up at Justine Manor were made up of intense study. Books were my world. Since I was not allowed to venture out of the grounds, they provided me with many adventures. Rarely was I allowed to play with other children. Charlotte's comfort and support became my sanity, and my imagination and love for writing became my best friend. My father had very little to do with me and never once tried to veil the scars he blamed me for. Occasionally I would be summoned to dine with him. Two places would be set at either end of the long mahogany table. I addressed my father as *Sir*. As the minutes ticked by, and each course was served, I would avoid looking up at his face, terrified that for a split second he might read the enmity I carried in my heart for his selfishness.

His pale, almost waxen, complexion made him appear sinister, yet at the same time he was a handsome man, tall, dark, and athletically slim. He dressed impeccably, but never wore anything that lifted his stern, stiff manner. Though my mother had long passed away, my father had continued to wear his wedding ring. One thing that struck me as strange was the large ruby ring he wore on the third finger of his right hand. It was so out of character for him to wear such a piece of ornate jewelry. As a young boy, I remember secretly gazing across the table at the mysterious large jewel that flashed like fire from his hand. I wanted to touch it, look at it closely. Yet I knew not to ask questions. That was not my place, and when dinner was over, I would be sent back to my room.

By the time I was eight years old, I had begun suffering from extreme nightmares about my father. His lack of love and constant rejection haunted my dreams with darkness and fear. I'd awake in fits of terror, crying and screaming to find Charlotte at my side trying to comfort me. The nightmares continued for a while, then slowly they occurred less and less. I can't remember when they stopped, but it seemed when they did, there was always something else to replace my hauntings.

As my adolescent years arrived, I had become accustomed to pain and numb to its torment. Tears did not help. My prayers were not answered, and it became clear to me that my father was never going to change. Everything about him was a mystery. His long trips away from home that no one spoke about. The days he'd spend alone when he'd return. Though I never heard him be rude or act mean to the servants, they all feared him. And so did I. His presence was powerful, silent and strong. A brilliant solicitor, respected and honored, but to me he still remained a heartless, cruel, man.

I spent my seventeenth birthday with Charlotte and as always she tried to make it special. My father was away, so I continued to work on my first novel. I dreamed of one day becoming a successful writer, a dream I decided to keep to myself. I wanted nothing more than to leave Justine Manor and prayed that my book might make that happen. I managed to finish it that same month. My father was still away, so I ventured into the city to deliver my work to a handful of publishers.

London overflowed with energy. The people were different. The air was different. This was a city that embraced excitement. I imagined myself living there, away from all the negativity and fear I'd absorbed growing up. Charlotte could stay with me. I would take care of her. I'd have a place of my own that overlooked the Heath. Sinking back in my carriage, I dared to dream, and it felt wonderful. You could say that I was beginning to be rebellious, but I didn't see it that way. All I was doing was rejecting a life that was not good for me. As we drove back from the city, I watched the rain begin to fall. I thought about my father and what he would say the moment I told him I wanted to be a writer. The thought made me shiver. I could already visualize the distaste in his eyes. Still, that wasn't going to stop me from telling him the truth.

I arrived back at the house to find Charlotte waiting for me by the front door. Her eyes were red and swollen. When I asked her what was wrong, she began to weep. "Nicholas," she sobbed, "it's about your father. Something terrible has happened. I'm so sorry Nicholas."

I remember standing frozen in disbelief, as she held my hands and told me my father had passed away. He had died four days ago in Paris from pneumonia. Mr. Wakeman, my father's solicitor, received the telegram that morning. He was waiting in the sitting room to see me.

For a moment, I felt I was going to cry, but something inside me numbed my emotions.

I walked into the sitting room and saw Mr. Wakeman by the fireplace. The whole thing was so surreal. Trying to concentrate, I listened to what he had to say. He told me that my father's body was on its way home and that he would be taking care of all the funeral arrangements. Then he took an envelope from the inside of his jacket.

"This is for you, Nicholas," he said. "Your father requested I give this to you if anything ever happened to him." Mr. Wakeman sat forward noticing my uncomfortable reaction. "Nicholas", he spoke warmly. "Your father and I go back many years. I remember you as a young boy. I remember when you met my daughter Elena. You must have been about nine years old. You and Elena played for hours here in this very room whilst your father and I attended to business. Do you recall that day?"

"Yes," I answered. Mr. Wakeman paused for a moment reading between the lines of my obvious silence.

"Nicholas, I know your father wasn't the kind of man who expressed his emotions openly, but there was no doubt how much he loved you. I am not sure if you are aware of this, but when your mother passed away, your father made you the sole heir of his estate. I'll arrange for us to meet at your convenience after the funeral."

He shook my hand and expressed his condolences again. "Try and get some rest, and please do not worry. I will take care of everything."

After Mr. Wakeman left, I disappeared to my room. I needed to be alone. I sat on my bed staring at the envelope in my hands. I opened it carefully and began to read the note my father had left for me. It simply read:

To my son Nicholas,
I have always loved you and hope that one day you will be able to forgive me. God bless you, my son. God bless your happiness.
Sincerely,
Your father, Edward.

As I read the note over and over again, a mountain of sorrow filled my chest. Why couldn't he have told me this when he was alive? All I had ever wanted was for my father to love me. Now it was too late, much too late. I wept.

I remember at the funeral feeling numb as I watched my father's coffin being lowered into the ground. I wanted to cry, I wanted to feel like his son, but the shame of his rejection had left me feeling like a fool. I was a stranger at my own father's funeral. Everyone around me knew him better than I. That day no tears fell down my sunken cheeks, but inside my heart my tears fell like rain.

When we arrived back at the house, I managed to escape a roomful of people I did not know. I sat on the back steps of Justine Manor, wishing they'd all just leave and disappear. It was then I heard a soft sweet voice I did not recognize behind me. Turning around, I saw a beautiful girl staring like an angel beneath the gray winter sky.

"Hello, Nicholas", she said quietly. "I hope you don't mind, but I wanted to see you before leaving. I'm so sorry about your father."

I looked up at her, wondering how she knew me. She smiled gently. "You don't remember me. I am Elena Wakeman. My father is Charles Wakeman. The last time I saw you, we were nine years old."

"Of course," I answered, taken by her beauty. I stood up to greet her. "Please forgive me. It's been a long time."

Elena smiled calmly as if she knew me, and as strange as it seemed I sensed maybe she did. From that moment on, it seemed destined that she and I would meet again. The more I spoke to her, the more I wanted her. I set out to see her again that week, and when I did, I set out to marry her. Her fiery red hair and emerald green eyes were as vibrant as the morning sun. I didn't know how I was going to win her heart, but that wasn't going to stop me from trying.

For the next few weeks, I tried to come to terms with the strange and difficult emotions I felt for my father. Losing him had changed something inside of me. I missed him deeply, yet at the same time I felt cheated and angry because he'd told me he loved me after he'd died. There were no warm memories for me to cling to, not one treasured moment with my father to remember. The last time I saw Elena's father, Mr. Wakeman, he had given me my father's ruby ring. He told me my father had left strict instructions that I should put it in the family safe. I guessed that he had presumed that I would never want to wear something of his, but he was wrong. His ring was his only possession that mattered to me. It was personal, priceless, and it helped remind me that I was my father's son.

After his death, a weird and dark emptiness hung over Justine Manor, and it wasn't long before even more darkness and grief made its way through its walls. Charlotte received news that her sister had passed away suddenly. I offered to take her to the funeral in Nottingham, but she insisted it was best she went alone.

Walking her down to the carriage, I held her hand just as she had held mine when I was a child. Her blue wintercoat was buttoned up to her scarf, her tired soft eyes adrift in sorrow. Before she left, she placed a small wooden box in my hand. "This is for you, Nicholas," she said. I've been meaning to give you this since your father's funeral."

I opened the box to find a gold cross and chain. Filled with emotion, I relived the moment when Charlotte had given me my first Bible when I was five years old. She had taught me the Lord's Prayer. She had taught me to believe in God. This was something that would have infuriated my father, for he was a non-believer. Crucifixes and Bibles belonged in churches, not in Justine Manor.

Charlotte hugged me tightly. "Keep safe," she said. "And do not worry about me. I'll be fine."

As the sun spread its veins of gold though the heavy gray clouds, I watched the coach pull away and prayed Charlotte would return home safely. The news about her sister had left me thinking about my father.

I sat at my desk trying to ignore the clock's irritating hands that ticked loudly with an air of defiance. I walked to the hearth, then back to my desk. Back to the hearth, back to my desk, back to the hearth, back to my desk. It was no good. I couldn't settle. I decided to visit my father's grave for the first time since his funeral. As my thoughts blew like lost leaves across a cold winter breeze, I reached the cemetery where both my mother and father were laid to rest. I stared down at my parents' graves and hoped that maybe they could hear my prayers. The weathered white angel that blessed my mother's grave gazed down with a silence that seemed to whisper my name. I brushed away the dead leaves that had gathered at her feet wanting to believe it wasn't my imagination. For a moment, I visualized everything that could have been, and for a moment, I felt like I belonged. Wiping the dirt from my mother's name, I exhaled my pain and whispered goodbye. Maybe now my father had found peace. Maybe now he could surrender his paper shield to the wind and fly like a warrior to my mother's side. Dipping my head, I closed my eyes.

In the name of the Father, and of the Son, and of the Holy Spirit, Amen.

CHAPTER TWO

MY AWAKENING

Christmas passed without any snow. I had seen Elena before she left to visit her aunt in Brighton for the holidays. Charlotte had not yet returned home. Her aunt had insisted she stay an extra week.

Though a whirlwind of change had left me astray, I'd began to accept that it was time to move on. My dream of having Elena was becoming a reality. The afternoons we had spent together proved more than just a casual friendship. We were drawn to each other, destined to be together. There was no doubt in my mind that she knew how much I loved her, but I needed to be patient. I didn't want to rush her. I knew she was coming home the following week; only seven days, but it seemed so long. Trying to relax, I flicked through the newspaper and noticed something that caught my attention, an article about a small traveling fair in Whitechapel that some were calling a devil's circus. The police were considering closing it down due to reports about some disturbing sideshows that were leaving audiences shaken and confused. I had to see this, I thought. True or false, it sounded like a great storyline for my next book.

That evening, I ventured into the city. I didn't want my personal driver knowing my whereabouts, so I asked that he take me to Covent Garden. From there, I'd continue alone. I waited for him to pull away and then crossed the street to where a hooded driver sat waiting for his next customer.

Climbing in, I asked, "There's a small traveling fair in Whitechapel. Have you heard about it?"

The driver only nodded and set off without the slightest hesitation. I assumed he must have known where it was. Eager and excited, I couldn't wait to get there and discover what all the commotion was about. The doors of the old coach rattled. The once-red velvet seats were now practically thread bare and proved to be very uncomfortable as we made our way across the bumpy dark streets. I checked my watch. We'd been traveling for nearly an hour. I began to feel nervous as I recognized that I was now completely lost. Maybe this wasn't such a good idea. I leaned forward. "Driver, how much longer?"

He didn't respond. I heard a noise in the distance. Someone was playing a piano. People were singing and yelling. It sounded like we were approaching a crowded tavern. As the noise became louder, it quickly faded leaving only a haunting silence. A deep panic stirred in my stomach. I stared out onto the damp, empty streets. The smell of cheap perfume settled upon the chilly stale air as we slowly passed some dimly lit alleyways. Young girls stood and provoked the night. Shamelessly, they offered themselves, flaunting their bosoms and lifting their unwashed petticoats. I sat back in my seat, uneasy and awkward. I had never seen anything like this before. Where the hell was I?

Then the loud echoing of horses' hooves stopped. We had come to a halt.

"Driver, where are we?" I asked. At that moment, a blanket of fog began covering the doors and windows of the carriage. Desperate to leave, I offered the driver all my money, shouting for him to take me back. Again he didn't answer. Climbing forward, I banged on the roof. "Can you hear me?" I yelled. "Please answer me!"

As the fog lifted, I realized the driver had gone. I'd been left alone in some back street from hell. I sat back on the seat, clutching the collar of my cloak as if it were a rope that could pull me out of this horrible nightmare. All at once, I heard a tap on the window, and through the mist, I saw a girl's face. Relieved to see someone, I opened the door. With a childlike innocence, the girl looked at me. Her long black hair fell loose over her shoulders. She clutched a red shawl that covered her white nightdress.

"Are you lost?" she asked.

"Yes," I answered. "I need to get back to Covent Garden. Do you know where I can find another driver?"

Her large dark eyes glistened unnaturally. "Yes," she answered. "Do not worry. I have a friend who can take you back. Come with me. I do not live far from here."

I began following her down the desolate street. The mysterious mist had now disappeared, but all I could think about was getting home. She led me down a long narrow alley where the smell of damp rotting wood turned my stomach.

"We are almost there." She took my hand then turned and continued across a small churchyard and down some steps to a narrow arched door.

"You live here?" I asked.

"Yes," she answered. "I work for the church. Father Hayden lets me stay here."

Inviting me inside a candlelit room, she asked me to sit. I looked around, nervously waiting. Then, I began to notice some of the strange unusual ornaments and paintings she had stored in one corner of the room. Beside her bed was an old worn dressing table holding a large gold mirror trimmed with colorful jewels. The stones looked authentic, but how could they be? This poor girl was living in a room without windows.

She knelt beside me and gave me some wine. I didn't want to drink it, but at the same time I didn't want to offend her.

"What is your name?" I asked.

"Odessa," she answered.

As she moved her hair away from her face, I noticed she was quite beautiful. I drank the red wine. It tasted unusually thick and heavy. "Will your friend be here soon?" I asked.

She nodded. "Yes. He will be here very soon."

As soon as I finished the wine, I began to feel dizzy. The room began to sway. My knees became weak. "Are you all right?" she asked.

Trying to pull myself together, I realized I could not stand.

"Let me help you," she said. "Come lie on my bed. You look tired."

Feeling disorientated, I let her help me to the bed. I needed to lie down. She rested my head against the cushioned headboard, then sat at her dresser and began brushing her long black hair. Still light headed, I watched her admire herself in the mirror.

"Tell me, Nicholas," she said. "What do you think brought you here tonight?"

I didn't remember telling her my name, and I didn't understand the meaning of her question. "What do you mean?" I asked, still unable to stand.

"Come, now, Nicholas." She smiled. "You must know that your being here with me is no coincidence."

I tried to sit forward. "I'm sorry, but I have no idea what you are talking about," I answered.

She turned on her stool to face me. "How is Elena?"

My heart began beating nervously. "How do you know her?"

She smiled arrogantly. "I know everything about Elena, just as I know everything about you."

"What is going on? Who are you? What do you want?" I began to panic.

She stood up as if she were a queen stepping off her throne. "I am the answer to your destiny, Nicholas. I am here to grant your wish."

I moved back on the bed as she began to walk toward me. "What are you? Some kind of witch? Please, all I want is to get back home."

Climbing onto the bed, she stared into my eyes. "I am not a witch, Nicholas. I am what every mortal would long to be. I am a vampire."

I didn't understand anything she was saying. I had never heard of a vampire before. Pulling the ribbon on her nightdress loose, she let it fall off one of her breasts. I was terrified, yet at the same time, aroused. I had never seen a naked woman before. She gazed at me with untamed eyes.

"Nicholas, you are here because you followed your instincts. You must follow the path that bears your name."

I looked back at her, captured by her presence, her voice. Her eyes were making me want her. She stroked her fingers through my hair and whispered, "Close your eyes. Imagine Elena, her lips, her kiss."

Entrapped by her powers, I closed my eyes and, like magic, I felt Elena was there. Her soft smooth breasts pressed against my chest. Her red, full lips tasted as sweet as honey. I opened my eyes and saw her face. "Elena," I said. "Is it really you?"

"Yes, Nicholas," she answered, kissing my neck. For a moment, I believed Elena was really there. It felt so real. I couldn't think straight. As I began to caress her perfect body, she whispered her desire into my ear. "Give me your soul Nicholas, and I am yours forever. Tell me your soul belongs to me."

Lost in a haze of pleasure and lust, I answered, "My soul is yours, my soul is yours until the end of time."

All at once her grip tightened as she forced my head to one side and bit deep into my neck. Thrown out of her spell, I tried to break free. But like a rabid dog, she wouldn't let go. I tried to scream and shake her off. She was stronger than I, drinking my blood while I lay there helpless. Then I felt her jaws unlock and saw Odessa's hideous face gazing down on me with flaming red eyes. Her canine teeth were dripping with my blood. Petrified, I dared not move as she turned away and sat in front of her dresser.

Brushing her long hair, she began babbling and giggling to herself like a possessed, mad child. Dizzy and weak, I slid off the bed watching her become lost in her own demonic world. She cast no reflection in the mirror. My heart thumped violently.

"Please God," I prayed. "Help me get away." Reaching for the door, I tried not to breathe. Then, pulling it open, I ran for my life. The last I remember, I was scrambling across the churchyard trembling with shock, desperate for help. I remember collapsing, hitting my face on the freezing cobblestones. Then I must have lost consciousness.

I never did discover how I got back to Justine Manor. When I awoke the next morning, I found myself lying on my bed. My shirt was torn and covered with blood, my hands, grazed and filthy from last night's escape. I shrieked in agony as I moved my head.

"God, my neck!" It hurt so much. Dragging myself up, I checked my wounds. They were deep and nasty. Two large punctures on the side of my neck made it look as though I'd been bitten by a large, savage dog. "Dear God," I said, under my breath. "What have I done?"

I pictured Odessa's demonic face, her canine teeth dripping with my blood. She had asked for my soul, and I had offered it to her. I was a victim of a satanic attack, an attack that no one in their right mind would believe. How could I expect the police to believe that I'd been bitten by a girl that had changed into a monster? She said she was a vampire. If such a word existed, I had to find out what it meant. I tried to clean the wounds on my neck. The pain was excruciating as I dabbed alcohol onto the bite. Managing to cover the seeping wounds, I scrubbed my body, desperately wanting to erase last night's nightmare.

Downstairs in the library, I searched for an answer. From morning to dusk, I continued to scan numerous books. I read about witches, warlocks and demons, spells and potions. The powers of evil, the power of human blood. Everything was there except the answer I needed. Exhausted, I rested at my father's desk. I thought back to the countless hours he had worked in this room. He had spent his life defending clients who vowed they were innocent, and he had never lost a case. A storm of fear turned in my stomach.

"Am I innocent?" I asked myself. "Or have I truly given my soul to the devil?"

Not even my father could have saved me from this. Whatever the outcome, I knew I was guilty. I sat, head in hands, worried and afraid, biting my nails like a nervous child. Heavy-eyed and tired, I drifted for a moment, listening to the sound of the crackling fire that helped cover the solitary hands of the grandfather clock. Suddenly I was startled by a loud thump. I jumped back half-asleep, feeling an odd cool breeze pass the back of my neck. A large book had fallen off one of the shelves. Pulling myself up, I went to put it back. The book was unusual, its black velvet cover without a title. I looked up to where it had fallen, although I could have sworn I'd already checked all the books on that shelf. Curious of its contents, I flicked through it. *Illustrations of the human body.* A science book, I thought. I scanned some of the chapters. *"The heart and its principal blood vessels." "The circulation of the blood, arteries, veins and capillaries."* It was interesting, but not what I was looking for. Just as I was about to put it back, I noticed a small bookmark sticking out from the pages. I opened it and stared in disbelief.

Chapter 30: Vampires. Myth or Truth?

My heart raced as I began to read, and the more I read, the more terrified I became. Every word, every comma, every breath of its sickness jumped out from the page like the devil grasping my throat.

"Vampires survived on blood alone."

"Immortal creatures that roamed the night."

I thought about the red wine Odessa had given me and its unusual under-taste that may have been her blood. If what it said in this book were true, I too could become a vampire. "Oh God. No!" I panicked.

I turned the page to more hideous details and sketches. A vampire was capable of altering his appearance. Some could transform into wolves or large bats. The more fresh blood they consumed, the more powerful they became. Their dead bodies never decomposed. They could even appear younger and more alluring. I wanted to vomit. Last night I had kissed and caressed a vampire. Unable to go on, I slammed the book closed. Beads of sweat trickled down my forehead. What had I done? I had to be strong. That night, I prayed and begged for forgiveness.

"Deliver us from evil, for thine is the kingdom, and the power, and the glory, forever and ever."

CHAPTER THREE

My Darkest Dawn

*I*could never have conceived what was about to happen to me. I had begun a sentence worse than prison, worse than anything I could ever have imagined. In the last few hours, my life had become a maze of darkness. I found I could no longer walk in the sun. My eyes, my body, had become so sensitive to the light that it was too unbearable, too painful to even step into the daylight. My world had turned upside down.

After sleeping through the day, I awoke at night. I tried for three nights to control my senses, but last night I weakened and committed a hideous and ungodly act. Through the grounds of Justine Manor, I spotted a deer deep in the woods. Its slender neck reached up to the branches, and for a moment, I admired its innocence and beauty. My nocturnal vision had become so sharp that I could see it clearly in the black of night. It wasn't until it began moving away that suddenly I began to crave the animal's blood. A violent hunger fired inside of me. My conscience and my senses were no longer in control. Within seconds, I felt my feet lift off the ground. I was flying through the woods, twisting in and out of the trees. I struck down, landing on top of the deer and broke its neck with ease. My hands and teeth tore into its neck, ripping and tearing like a wild savage beast. The hot gaping flesh excited me while its blood, thick and warm, flooded my throat. Digging my fangs deeper and deeper into its neck, I drank. The more I drank, the stronger I felt. This blood, I realized, was my life force.

I drank until my stomach was full. Resting beside the dead animal, I didn't care that my hands were soaked in blood. Instead, I welcomed the rush of exhilaration that raced through my body. It wasn't until I began to feel normal again that suddenly I realized the hideous act I had committed. Finding myself lying on the cold damp grass I stared in disbelief at the lifeless deer. I could still taste its blood, still smell its raw flesh on my face and neck. Tears flooded my eyes, and I begged and pleaded to be released from this curse.

"Please God, save me. I did not do this. This is not me," I kept on repeating.

Forks of lighting began punishing the ground as if the heavens were answering me with an almighty roar. Afraid and desperate, I ran back through the rain and entered the house through the cellar where no one could see me. I made it back to my room and scrubbed myself clean. My heart pounded as I tried to think of a way to get rid of this curse. Suddenly it hit me. I had to go back to Whitechapel. I had to find Odessa. Her vampire powers had done this to me. She was the only one who could undo this spell.

Quickly and quietly, I left the house and returned to Whitechapel believing I could end my nightmare. I searched every churchyard, every street, every tavern, every alley, but there was nothing. No clues. Not one sign of hope. Odessa had vanished.

That week I realized there was nothing I could do to change what was happening to me. The sun was my enemy. I couldn't eat. I couldn't drink anything but blood or red wine. My world began at sundown and, as much as I tried to fight my craving for more blood, it worsened. Not wanting to, feeling I had no choice, I hunted deep in the woods again. Every night I still thought about Elena and how much I still desired her. I knew it was beyond all reason to think that she could still love me, but that didn't stop my heart's decision.

The next week, I arranged to meet with Elena at her home in Hampstead. Seeing her again was like seeing the sunrise. She was the light out of my darkness, and by the way she greeted me, I was sure she'd missed me. We spoke about her trip, her aunt, and her family. God, she was beautiful. Those eyes, that smile, her silky red hair. I yearned to make love to her now and forever. To my relief, she didn't seem to notice anything different about me. Her affection was genuine. So much so that I had to control my desperate desire to kiss her. It wasn't until I held her hand that I was able to feel that something was troubling her. It was as if she were hiding a difficult dilemma, an unanswered question that was making her sad. She looked at me and stroked my cheek tenderly.

"Nicholas, what are you thinking about?"

"You," I whispered. "Only you." For the first time, our lips met. Then suddenly the drawing room door opened, and Mr. Wakeman strode in.

"Nicholas," he said, "how good to see you." Walking over, he shook my hand. As he sat down, I immediately noticed a tension in the air. The more he made conversation, the more irritated and upset Elena became. Pouring himself a drink, he continued. "Has Elena told you the wonderful news?"

Elena stood up overcome with emotion. "I'm not going to marry Mark, Father," she said, and stormed out the room.

Mr. Wakeman turned back to me. "Do not look so worried, Nicholas." He smiled casually. "It's only pre-wedding nerves. Elena is just being a typical bride. Mark Ludwick's a fine young man, a perfect match for her. He and his family visited us in Brighton over Christmas. He asked for Elena's hand in marriage, and she accepted. Elena knows what's right for her. She knows she is doing the right thing."

I sat completely thrown by Mr. Wakeman's lack of compassion. It was obvious Elena did not love this man, and there was no way I was going to let anyone steal her from me. Before I left that night, I slipped a note inside her hand.

"I love you," I wrote. *"Please meet with me tomorrow at midnight on the corner of your street. I can't let you marry someone else, but there is something I must tell you – something important."*

That was all I could do for now. If Elena felt the same way, I was sure she'd be there.

The next evening, my hunger returned, and again I hunted deep in the woods. Back at the house, I thought and thought about how I was going to explain my nocturnal curse to Elena. Becoming a vampire hadn't changed the way I thought or what I believed in. It was all wrong. Horribly wrong. Drinking the blood of animals was my only way of survival, but that didn't make it any less horrific. I knew I couldn't bring myself to tell Elena the whole truth, but I still had to tell her that I was unable to face the daylight.

At midnight, I waited at the end of her street, and to my relief, Elena came out to meet me. I could see she'd been crying as we kissed and stepped up into my carriage. She held my hands like a helpless child.

"Nicholas," she whispered. "I don't know what to do. My father refuses to listen to me. I tried telling him today that I do not want to marry Mark, but nothing I say changes his mind. I love my father dearly, but this time he is asking too much of me."

"What about your mother?"

"She always agrees with my father. It's as if she doesn't have a mind of her own. Please, Nicholas," she pleaded, "If you love me, take me away from all this. I'll go anywhere with you. I love you."

As I held her in my arms, I knew I had to tell her the truth, but I couldn't chance losing her. I had no choice but to lie.

"Elena," I said. "You know how much I love you, but there is something about me you need to know. I have developed a rare skin condition that cannot be healed. I am allergic to sunlight. For the past two weeks, my world has become a nocturnal nightmare."

Elena paused, her eyes filled with compassion. "Are you sure there is nothing the doctors can do to help you?"

"I am sure," I answered, "and I understand if you no longer want to be with me."

"How can you say that, Nicholas? I love you. I want to be with you." She kissed me. "Night or day, my heart is still yours. Nothing can change that. Nothing."

Gazing into her eyes, I couldn't believe her devoted response. "Then tomorrow, if you wish, we could leave for Paris."

"Yes, yes," she answered. "I will come to your house at sunset. No matter what, I will be there."

I watched her hurry back down the street and disappear inside the gates of her house. For the first time since becoming a vampire, I was able to put aside the horror of my curse. All I could think about was Elena. She was my only true reason to fight through the sins and torment of my own mistake.

Leaving Justine Manor was no hardship for me. In fact, it made sense to get away and start afresh somewhere else. I had read about the beauty of Paris. The fact that my father had died there didn't change my heart's choice.

Elena arrived the next evening, as she had promised, and we left for Paris, carrying two small suitcases and a mountain of dreams. Some might have said we were selfish and irresponsible, but we didn't see it that way. For we were in love.

We found a beautiful, large three-story townhouse that overlooked the Champs' Elysees. Elena was happier than I'd ever seen her. She adored Paris, and I adored her. My insecurity of knowing I was an inexperienced lover had passed. Being a vampire had given me the gift to make love to her with a passion and depth I had never imagined. Every night I worshipped her. Every night was bliss.

It was only until I left her bedside that my heaven would throw me back into hell. I hunted on the outskirts of the city, deep in the countryside where the wild life was abundant and easy prey. It seemed my powers were growing stronger. I was able to sense danger. I could recognize the fear, love, and hate in people's eyes, smell their innocence and identify their guilt. Though sometimes I found it incredibly hard to control my craving for human blood, I didn't succumb. It was punishingly difficult, but I didn't do it. Elena was my biggest challenge. Everything about her aroused my senses. Her smell, her touch, her taste. It was agonizing to balance a vampire's love with a human heart, but I loved her too much to ever make her a vampire.

Our first month in Paris had passed. My dream of having Elena was now a reality, but the fear of losing her still played on my mind constantly. While I slept through the day in my windowless room on the lower floor of the house, she was left to wander alone unprotected. This didn't seem to worry her. She never complained or made me feel inadequate; in fact she made sure to tell the servants not to disturb me during the day. Many times I'd awake to find another unknown artist's work hung on the wall. Some might have described Elena's individualism and taste as a little eccentric, but to me it expressed the fire in her soul. She was everything a man could wish for in a woman, yet at the same time, she was as innocent and trusting as a child.

Most evenings, we visited the St. Germain quarter, where poets and artists ignited the air with a sensuality and romance that made the young and old feel immortal. We dined regularly at the Café de Rouge. The small round tables dressed with red tablecloths and empty wine bottles used for burning long red candles flowed with the Bohemian spirit of the writers and locals who ate there.

Elena never asked why I did not eat with her. She believed my reasons for not feeling hungry and assumed I ate later when she was sleeping. While she sipped champagne, I drank my red wine. Together we'd enjoy the heartfelt talents of the old violinist who played regularly in the square. Being surrounded by nocturnal musicians, philosophers, painters, and writers made me feel comfortable. Their world of imagination breathed at night. I had found an area where I could return and relax until the early hours. No one asked questions. No one bothered me. I could sit alone undisturbed and leave unobtrusively before sunrise.

The more I discovered about Paris, the more I began to understand another side to my father. He had spent so much time here that it became obvious to me that he must have enjoyed this beautiful city. Although I doubted that his trips had to do with business, that didn't matter now. I just felt good imagining my father as being a more exciting and colorful person than the man I remembered.

Elena had written to her mother and father numerous times but still hadn't received a reply. For her sake, I hoped they'd soon be in touch. If not, I felt it was my responsibility to pay her father a visit and make the peace. I wanted to marry Elena. In order to do that, I wanted to explain to Mr. and Mrs. Wakeman how much I loved their daughter. Right now, however, Elena had asked me to wait. She was convinced her father would write back to her before long, and that when he did, everything would be all right.

Another month passed, and still no word. Elena insisted that I not visit her father.

"My parents know where I am," she said. "They know I love them. I have nothing to feel guilty about."

She was right. There was no reason for her to feel guilty. I only wished I could have felt the same. Lying to her about my nocturnal world had been easy in the beginning, but continuing to lie to her was becoming more difficult by the day. I loved her so much that it killed me to hide the truth from her. I was a vampire who worshipped the ground she walked on. I was a sinner who had stolen an angel. I had hoped God would forgive me for my selfishness. But God only knew, I just couldn't let her go.

CHAPTER FOUR

⁓

TWO LOVERS IN PARIS

*H*ow I wished I could have shared the magic of an April sunrise with the woman I loved. Losing the mornings of a God-given gift when spring unveils its virginal beauty only reminded me of what I had become. The sounds of the birds singing at daybreak, a kiss in the sun, a walk in the park, such simple pleasures that lovers experience together. Yet, for me, they had become my priceless loss. I continued to go back and re-read the same chapter about vampires in the book I had found in my father's library. I had brought it to Paris with me, hidden in my suitcase like some dark secret journal. It was my only source of information that helped me understand the change to my existence. Most of what it explained had already happened to me. But still there were secrets that remained almost inconceivable to me and being immortal was one of them. As much as I wanted to disbelieve it, I couldn't. If there was one lesson I had learned since becoming a vampire, it was that anything is possible. I was living proof of that. The powers I had been given made me view the world with different eyes. I was aware of its shadows and ghostlike forces. Ideas I had once perceived as fictitious and contrary to reason, I now realized were not beyond the bounds of possibility. My only link to a normal life was having Elena to love and cherish. Maybe in some strange way God had shown me mercy by giving me hope through Elena's eyes. I wanted to believe that. I needed to believe it.

The bitter truth hit me the night I received a letter from Nottingham. It was from Charlotte's brother-in-law, dated over six weeks ago. I was devastated to learn that Charlotte had been in a tragic accident. She had left Nottingham and was traveling back to Essex when a terrible storm had broken out. Her driver had lost control, and Charlotte had been thrown from the carriage, and had fallen beneath one of its wheels. She died almost instantly. Trying to read through a veil of tears, I was frozen in shock, unable to accept that Charlotte was dead. I felt I was dreaming, desperate to wake up. When was this ongoing nightmare ever going to end? Collapsing at my desk, I could hardly breathe as I tried to imagine my life without her.

I had written to Charlotte and invited her to come to Paris. She was planning to visit us and stay for the summer. Holding the letter, I wept like a child as a lifetime of memories passed before me.

Charlotte had been like a mother to me. She had brought me up, given me support. Without her guidance and affection, I would never have known the meaning of love or God. I remembered the last time we said goodbye, remembered the cross and chain she had given me before leaving for Nottingham. I had brought it to Paris with me, still in its box, still unworn. Taking the box from my desk drawer, I opened it and let the necklace drop into my hand. Suddenly, I felt a burning pain, forcing me to let go. Then I realized the shattering truth. I saw the sign of God's rejection. The cross had burned its mark into my palm. Jumping up, I lost all control and shouted like a mad man, smashing everything in sight.

"Why me?" I screamed. "Why are you doing this to me? I didn't choose to become a vampire! I didn't want this to happen to me."

Suddenly Elena came rushing into the room. "Nicholas, what is wrong? What are you doing?"

I turned away from her. "Leave. Just leave."

"Nicholas," she said. "Tell me what's wrong."

Too upset to think, I couldn't control my rage. "Go away," I yelled. "You cannot stay here. You have to leave. Please just go."

"But Nicholas . . ."

"You don't understand. If you knew the truth, you'd know I'm trying to protect you." Feeling my world crumbling around me, I sat and wept.

Elena came to me. "It's all right, Nicholas. It's all right," she whispered.

"It's not," I wept. "If only it were. I've been lying to you, Elena. I've been too scared to tell you the truth."

"The truth about what?" she asked.

"About everything." I focused my gaze on her, looked into her eyes. "I am a vampire. I've been cursed, and there is nothing I can do to reverse the spell."

"What spell, Nicholas? You're not making sense."

"None of it makes sense," I said, "but you have to believe me. I'm telling you the truth. Tonight I received news that Charlotte died six weeks ago. There was an accident, a horrible accident. When I tried to hold the cross she gave me, it burned my hand. I could not pray. I've been damned to hell."

Opening my hand, I showed her the mark. Elena stared in disbelief. "How did this happen? I'll fetch a doctor."

"No," I yelled. For a moment, Elena stood in shock, not knowing what to say or do. Her eyes filled with tears.

"I'm so sorry Nicholas," she said. "I'm so sorry about Charlotte." As she tried to comfort me, more and more dread hit my stomach.

"I know this sounds ludicrous Elena, but I can't help feeling that somehow I'm to blame for Charlotte and my father's death. Everyone I love has been taken away. I'm beginning to believe my whole life has been ill-fated, and now it's becoming one tragedy after another. "

"Don't say that. It's not your fault."

"Maybe you're right," I answered, "but I don't know anymore. I became a vampire because of one innocent mistake. A mistake that has cost me the loss of my soul.

There are things you don't know about me, ungodly things I cannot control."

"What things, Nicholas? What are you talking about? You said you've been cursed. Who has cursed you?"

Asking her to sit, I began to explain the horrific details of what happened the night I was attacked. I went on to show her the book I had found in my father's library and opened it to the chapter that described vampires. Elena sat silent and began to read. She didn't look up. She didn't comment, but as she wiped the tears from her cheeks, I knew that the truth was beginning to sink in. It wasn't until she closed the book that her silence became deafening clear.

I waited for her to tell me she was going to leave me. Her soft worried eyes reached out to me from across the room.

"Nicholas, I can't stop loving you. Whatever it takes, however difficult our lives become, I'm not going back to London. I want to stay here with you."

Her words shocked me, and they also made me fearful. "How do I know that what you feel is true?" I asked her. "Sometimes my emotions make things happen. I have been given certain powers that I have not yet fully learned to control. That night I asked you to come to Paris, I don't know if I hypnotized you. All I know is that I wanted you so much, I'd have done anything to have you."

"You didn't hypnotize me," she said. "I knew I was in love with you before I left for Brighton. When Mark Ludwick asked for my hand in marriage, all I wanted was to be with you."

"Oh Elena, my love, I don't want you to suffer for my mistakes. As much as I fight what has happened to me and avoid human blood, I cannot trust who I am anymore. If I weaken, I'll become nothing more than a murderer, a monster."

"You won't weaken, and you'll never be a monster."

"I pray you're right, but how can I be sure? Think about what I'm saying. This isn't a fairy tale. There is no happy ending Elena. Tomorrow when I wake up and find you gone, I will understand, and I will always love you." Taking her in my arms, I kissed her goodbye and watched her walk to the door.

"Nicholas." She turned to me. "I will follow my heart, not your demands."

Saying nothing, I treasured every breath of every moment I had spent loving her. Elena had given me a piece of heaven, but I knew by tomorrow that heaven would end.

That tomorrow never came to pass, at least not then. As much as I'd tried to convince Elena to leave me, she remained like an angel by my side. Telling her the truth turned out to be the key that unlocked the door to my freedom. I was able to love her as never before. I was her vampire, and she was my life. Together, our journey became an unyielding bond, an unpredictable love affair that created a world of unstoppable passion. I had the powers to give her more than any mortal could ever dream of giving her, and for the first time I let her experience that magic. Whatever nightmares I had to deal with, I dealt with them alone. She was my reason, my conscience, my guide. Elena had climbed a mountain of choices to be with me, and I wasn't about to let go of her hand.

As the weeks passed, I learned to accept the pain and anger that came with losing Charlotte and my father. I tried to look forward without fear or regret. When Elena told me she had befriended an old widow, Countess Katherine Boucher, across the square, I was pleased. She had someone to visit, I thought, someone to spend a rainy afternoon with. She described the Countess as being a kind, generous lady that made her feel more like a granddaughter than a friend. This concerned me, but still I said nothing. Apparently the Countess and her late husband had been childless, which probably explained her behavior.

I was further troubled when I noticed Elena wearing a necklace Countess Boucher had given her. It was a large gold locket containing some unusual herb. When I asked Elena why she was wearing it, she explained that Madame Boucher was a member of an elite private astrology club. The necklace was meant to be a symbol of good luck. I asked Elena to take it off.

"Come now," she teased. " It's only a necklace. I know it's unusual, but I rather like it."

"I'm not joking," I said firmly. "I don't want you to wear it."

Elena's eyes dropped like a scorned child's. "All right." She sighed. "If it displeases you that much, I'll take it off."

I picked it up to take a closer look at the unfamiliar dried herb inside the locket. It didn't carry a strong odor, and the locket did look somewhat expensive.

"Why are you studying it like that?" Elena asked. "It's just a gift."

"Yes," I answered now questioning why the old widow felt Elena needed something to bring her good luck. "So she studies astrology? Have you told her much about us?"

"Yes, of course," Elena answered. "I told her you are a writer and how much I love you. Oh Nicholas..." She began to laugh. "Stop being so distrustful. She knows nothing about our secret. She's just a helpless old lady who wants to be friends with both of us. She asked if we could stop by to see her this evening. She'd love to meet you. Please say yes."

"Very well," I said, if only to ease my doubts. Though it seemed ridiculous that I should question a harmless old woman's gift, I couldn't help it. What had happened to me had left me a skeptic. I mistrusted surprises, I mistrusted the world. Be it wrong or right, that's the way it was.

Meeting the Countess did not ease my suspicions. From the moment she greeted us, I felt her scrutinizing my every move. She sat waiting in a tall, almost throne-like red velvet chair by the fire smoking a long, thin black cigar with the arrogance of a peacock. Her large round frame filled her chair.

"Please sit," she said pointing to the sofa beside her. I couldn't see why Elena had described her as being helpless. She came off as being completely the opposite. Turning to me, she said, "I am so glad you came, Nicholas. Elena has told me so much about you. I hear you are a writer. How thrilling that must be. Elena is very proud of your work."

I looked at Elena feeling uncomfortable. "She is being far too generous about my work," I said, trying to steer the conversation somewhere else.

"I like that," the Countess said, laughing. "Modesty, a rare commodity." Lighting another cigar she asked one of her servants to fetch some champagne. "Have you a publisher yet, Nicholas?"

"No, not yet," I answered.

"Well, maybe I could help. I know one or two people in the publishing business.

I nodded politely, not saying a word.

"So." The Countess smiled, stroking the long string of pearls that hung around her short, chubby neck. "I'm so glad you don't mind visiting an old lady like me."

"Do not say that, Katherine. I love hearing about all the exciting places you've visited and your interest in astrology." Elena paused awkwardly, realizing she wasn't wearing the locket. The Countess read Elena's unease.

"Oh, don't be embarrassed, child." The Countess smiled. "I understand if you don't like the necklace."

"Oh but I do. I do," Elena insisted.

"Then you should wear it, my dear. Like I told you before, it will bring you good luck," she said, noticing my silence.

Something about the old woman bothered me much more than her pushy personality. I tried to read what she was thinking, but for some strange reason, I couldn't. This puzzled me. Since becoming a vampire, I had developed an ability to read most people's thoughts when I chose to, if only for a few seconds. There was only one person I never dared to read, and that was Elena. For I feared that I might learn that I had failed her.

The Countess shuffled back into her chair. "I have something for the two of you," she continued. "Nicholas, would you be so kind as to pass me that small box on the table behind you."

Passing her the box, I noticed her eyes widen as she took out a gold envelope from a stack of letters.

"Here." She handed it to Elena.

"What is it?" Elena asked.

"Open it and see."

Elena opened the envelope carefully and pulled out an invitation. "Have you ever attended the opera ball in Versailles?"

"No," Elena answered with wonder.

"Nicholas?" She passed the fashionable invitation to me.

I could feel the Countess studying my every move. A sense of concern stirred inside of me as I read the invitation. It didn't feel right. In fact, everything about it felt wrong.

"Thank you so much," Elena told her.

"It is my pleasure, my dear. I know how much you both love Paris, but until you experience an evening like this, you truly have not lived. Of course you cannot purchase an invitation like this. One needs to be important enough to be invited."

Elena sat up straight. "What do you mean important?"

The old Countess laughed aloud, holding her long cigar up in the air.

"Extremely wealthy, my dear. Only the *creme de la crème* attends an event like this. Maurice, my late husband, and I loved going every year. Did you show Nicholas his portrait in the hall?"

"No. . ."

"Well, you'll see it on your way out. He was a handsome devil. There isn't a day that goes by that I don't think about him. When he passed away three years ago, I continued to attend on my own, but this year I am hoping you will both accompany me and make an old Countess happy."

"We'd be honored Katherine," Elena replied. "Wouldn't we, Nicholas?"

I immediately wanted to say no, but I could see how much this meant to Elena, and I didn't want to upset her.

The Countess smiled. "I shall make all the arrangements. The first thing we need to do is to have a dress made for you, Elena. I happen to know one of the best designers in the city. Leave it to me. You must come and see me tomorrow. We shall go there together."

Eager to leave, I stood up. "Well, Elena. I think it's time we were leaving. It's been a pleasure, Countess. I'm sure you and Elena can discuss all the details tomorrow."

The Countess stared with disapproval. "Forgive me for not standing, but my back's a little stiff today." She rang a small bell beside her chair. "James will see you out," she said.

Following the butler down the hall, I stopped to look at the portrait of her late husband. His sharp, heavy eyes peered down from the wall as if he were still alive, watching who came and went. I couldn't help noticing the large gold pendant he was wearing. It was engraved with some kind of ancient symbol. His left hand rested on his jacket pocket and bore a large gold ring with the same odd writing on it. For a split second I felt an inexplicable chill pass through me, and then suddenly, it stopped.

"Nicholas, are we leaving?" Elena whispered.

"Yes, of course." I took her hand and walked outside. As we made our way across town, I thought about Madam Boucher and her late husband. On the surface, they appeared to have been just a weird old couple dabbling in astrology, but I couldn't help wondering what they had to hide.

Elena kissed me. "I know what you are thinking." She smiled, "But don't misjudge Katherine just because she's a little strange. Once you get to know her, you'll like her. You'll see."

Our carriage slowed down, and it felt good to be back on the streets of St. Germain. As we strolled down the narrow streets past the lively cafes and heartfelt poets, I thought about what Elena had told Madame Boucher about me being a writer. It had struck a chord deep inside of me. Since becoming a vampire, my world had turned into a labyrinth of confusion. As grateful as I was to have Elena in my life, at the same time, I had let my dream of becoming a great writer slip away. I pictured myself back at Justine Manor as a boy lighting my candle late at night, writing stories that had helped me see beyond my loneliness—dreams of heroes and courageous warriors, a child's imagination that had carried me on horseback victoriously into the sunset. I knew in my heart it was wrong to let that go. I was a vampire, but beneath it all, I was still Nicholas, and I realized how important it was for me to find myself again.

Suddenly, Elena stopped me and pointed down a small side alleyway. "Isn't that the old violinist who plays in the square?"

I immediately recognized the old man sitting on a step, resting his head on a small shabby suitcase. "I believe it is," I said.

"He looks so lost, Nicholas. We haven't seen him playing in the square lately. I wonder if he is all right."

I asked Elena to wait a moment and walked down the alley to ask what was wrong. The old man was weeping, his hands clenching his cap.

"Excuse me." I spoke quietly, not wanting to scare him.

He looked up and wiped his eyes with his cap. "Yes?" he said, sniffing.

"I noticed you sitting here. You look very upset. Are you all right?"

The old man nodded nervously, saying nothing.

"You are the violinist who plays in the square?"

"Yes." He nodded. "I am."

"What is your name?" I asked.

"Francis."

"It is a pleasure to meet you, Francis," I said. "I am Nicholas Justine. My fiancée, Elena, and I have spent many evenings enjoying your music. We haven't seen you in the square lately. Has something happened? Do you need help?"

Again he wiped his tired eyes. The deep weary lines on his face suggested a lifetime of struggle. "Thank you for your concern," he said, "but there is nothing anyone can do to change anything now."

Wanting to help him, I continued. "I know I am just a stranger, but if you tell me what's troubling you, maybe I can help."

The old man looked up at me, his obvious heavy heart bearing his desperation. I heard his thoughts before he answered me. Everything had been taken from him,

"Where is your violin?" I asked. "Has someone stolen it?"

Struggling not to cry, he shook his head. "I have nothing anymore. Not even my violin," he lamented. "They have taken everything."

"Who?" I asked.

The family who owned the building I have lived in for the past forty years. I had a room there; it was my home. The last few months have been hard. I didn't earn enough. I didn't have enough to pay the landlord. Last week, I was turned out onto the street. They took the few possessions I had, including my violin." He paused, trying not to cry, "My violin is my keep. Without it, I cannot survive. I am an honest man. I have always paid my way. But now there is no hope. I have nothing left."

I gave him some money, but I wanted to do more for him.

"Thank you." The old man looked up at me. "I will never forget your kindness."

I picked up a handful of small stones and asked, "Open your cap, please."

He slowly did so, and I dropped them inside.

He closed his cap and gave me a quizzical look.

"Goodbye, my friend," I said. "Take care."

As I walked away, Elena rushed up to me. "Is he all right, Nicholas? Did you give him some money?"

"Yes," I answered. "God willing, he will be fine now."

As we began down the lane, we heard the old man call out, "Wait!"

Hurrying towards us, he held out his cap. "Thank you, thank you. Please wait," he called out. Holding out his cap, he showed me the stones. "They are emeralds," he gasped. "You turned the stones into emeralds. It is a miracle."

"Hush, my friend," I answered. "There is no need to thank me. Just go, be safe, and play your music."

That night was the first time I had used my powers to help someone. I felt like a pupil who had been given the tools of magic without the knowledge of how to control it. I wasn't sure how I had performed such a miracle. I was happy, and yet at the same time, I was scared. If my powers could do that when my heart felt compassion, what might they do if my heart felt hatred?

As we left the old man, Elena looked up with pride and adulation. "I love you Nicholas," she whispered. "Take me home my love, my vampire," she smiled.

Lifting her into my arms, I swept her above the empty street and together we flew across a moonlit sky. We kissed beneath the stars. Two hearts, one passion, one secret in the wind. That was our world. That was our sunset.

CHAPTER FIVE

THE BALL IN VERSAILLES

*I*t was nearing 7 pm. I sat back and sipped a little wine whilst I waited for Elena downstairs in the drawing room. That night we were leaving for the ball in Versailles. Madame Boucher had asked if we would travel with her, an arrangement I wished we could have avoided.

Elena appeared breathtakingly beautiful. Her long red hair was swept up and crowned beneath a black-jeweled tiara. A flowing red dress rested gently off her shoulders. She looked elegant and young, yet at the same time she was ravishingly stunning. Everything about Elena was different than other women. Her natural manner, her smile, her silence, her moods. She was an enigma, a mystery to be treasured. Taking a red rose from the vase beside me, I walked across the room and kissed her.

"Close your eyes," I whispered. She closed her eyes like an excited child as I let my emotions transform the rose into a precious jewel. "Here," I said. She opened her eyes and stared down at the ruby rose necklace.

"Oh Nicholas, it's beautiful," she gasped. "I've never seen anything so beautiful." Her eyes glistened as I placed it around her dainty neck. I wanted to make love to her, kiss every part of her perfect body, but I knew it was time to leave.

Outside, Countess Boucher waited in her carriage. "Come, my dear," she told Elena, shuffling herself up on her seat. "Sit here with me."

I got the feeling the Countess didn't like me very much, and I was sure she probably realized that the feeling was mutual.

"What an unusual necklace," she told Elena. " It is quite charming in an odd sort of way." Her thick fingers touched the ruby petals. "It looks almost like a real rose. Was it a gift?"

"Yes." Elena smiled, stroking it affectionately. "Nicholas made it for me."

"Made it?" The Countess chuckled sarcastically. "Don't you mean *gave* it to you, my dear?"

"Yes, of course," Elena answered, clearly uncomfortable.

"Did you buy it here in Paris, Nicholas?"

"No, it belonged to my mother."

"Ah, I see." She began smoking her long cigar. "I should have guessed that."

I ignored her obnoxious remark and watched her take out a small silver flask.

"Nothing like a drop of brandy to warm up," she said, sternly taking a large gulp. By the time we finally reached Versailles, I was already counting the hours to when we'd be able to return home. I couldn't have cared how spectacular the evening proved to be. The Countess was unbearable and became more and more so as the night proceeded.

Once inside the grand ballroom, she introduced us to some of her acquaintances. First came Charles Trembly, a heavyset middle-aged, pompous man who appeared to do nothing more than over-eat and drink. Grabbing another hors d'oeuvre from a passing tray, he stuffed it in his mouth and swallowed it whole. Countess Boucher introduced us, taking great pleasure in seeing Charles Trembly's greedy eyes light up as he gazed at Elena.

"The pleasure is all mine." He kissed Elena's hand. Looking back at me, he tried to be amusing. "I didn't quite catch your name," he said with a grin.

"Didn't you?" I asked coldly, not bothering to repeat it. Just then we were joined by another gentleman, a Professor Dalton.

"Ah, Professor," Trembly yelled. "I didn't expect to see you here. Did you leave the family back in London?" Before Professor Dalton had time to answer, Trembly added in a loud voice, "Peter has nine children. An expensive pastime, don't you think?"

The thin, tall professor grinned. "Yes, and thank God I have enough income to support them all."

Trembly gave a wicked chuckle. "Shouldn't you be thanking the devil instead?"

Professor Dalton gave an unsettled grin.

"Oh Charles," the Countess jumped in. "You're such a tease. Too much champagne already!" She grabbed another glass for herself.

Though the evening itself was a dashing affair, it was difficult for Elena and me to enjoy its splendor. I could see that she wanted to escape the Countess as much as I did.

Taking Elena's hand, I said, "Shall we dance?"

This was her evening, and I wanted her to have a good time. Leading her onto the floor, I noticed the curious stares of delight and envy. Elena was without a doubt the most enchanting woman in the room, fresh and innocent as a soft summer breeze. Beneath the glittering chandeliers, we shared a moment that helped erase an aggravating start to the evening.

Suddenly, she looked into my eyes, her face pale. "Could we sit down?"

"Are you all right?" I asked.

"Yes, do not worry. I'm fine." She smiled. I just feel a little nauseated."

"You need to eat something. I'll get you some food."

"No, Nicholas. I'm fine," she insisted. I have been feeling a little off for the past week, but it's usually in the morning."

"Have you seen a doctor?"

She paused, "Oh, Nicholas," she teased. "I was going to tell you when we got home, but I can't wait any longer. I found out only today."

"Found out what?"

"That we are going to have a child. Isn't it wonderful?"

"Are you sure?" I asked her.

"Of course I'm sure, Nicholas. Aren't you happy?"

"Yes, of course, I'm happy," I answered, trying to hide my concern and worry. I tried not to appear nervous and unsure. This should have been the greatest news of my life, but being a vampire had changed everything. How was I ever going to be a normal father?

"Nicholas. What's wrong? Aren't you pleased?" Elena asked uneasily.

"Nothing's wrong." I kissed her tenderly. Just then, I felt a tap on my shoulder.

"Is everything all right?" the Countess asked. "I saw you both dancing and then noticed you having to sit down, Elena."

Before Elena had a chance to say anything, I said, "Actually, I am the one who needed to sit."

"Really?" The Countess looked confused.

"Yes," I said, "I don't know why, but suddenly I felt dizzy."

"Um, strange," the Countess said, puffing her black cigar. Elena looked at me, aware of my decision not to share our news with her. "Well, when you are ready, I have someone else I'd like you both to meet. Why don't I take Elena to our table whilst you step outside and get a little fresh air, Nicholas? That will do you good."

"Maybe you should," Elena said, giving my hand a slight squeeze. "I'll wait at the table. Hurry back."

I went outside for a few minutes, and then quickly returned inside the ballroom. As I approached the table, I noticed a dark-haired distinguished-looking gentleman talking to Elena and the Countess. His hand brushed Elena's shoulder flirtatiously, making her blush and move back on her chair. Glaring down at him, I waited for him to move seats. He stood up and smiled, paying no attention to my reaction.

"Please allow me to introduce myself," he said. " I am Count Victor Du Fay." Seating himself across from Elena, he lit a cigar with an amused expression. His thick black hair was slicked back from his dark, dominant piercing eyes. He appeared to be in his late thirties and fairly handsome, but his manner revealed nothing more than his own self-importance.

Countess Boucher sat forward and raised her glass. "To my dear friends," she shouted over the music. "I have told Victor what a wonderful couple you are and how blessed I am to have you living across the square from me."

Count Du Fay smiled. "It seems you've made quite an impression on Katherine. She doesn't usually behave this kindly about anyone. Not even Maurice, her late husband," he joked.

Countess Boucher enjoyed Du Fay's teasing. She fluttered her eyelashes at him as if she were thirty years younger. "Why, I don't know what you mean," she said, almost swaying off her seat, slightly intoxicated.

Du Fay stared across at Elena as if he were admiring a fine portrait. He sipped his champagne and gave a worldly smile. "You are a lucky man, Mr. Justine. It is without question that you have the most beautiful girl here tonight."

Elena didn't respond to his flattery. Instead she asked, "Are you married, Count Du Fay?"

"No, unfortunately." He shook his head. "It seems all the finest women are taken."

Finding him increasingly irritating, I spoke up. "Paris is full of unmarried, attractive women."

"That may be true," he said, "but it all depends on how particular one is. It is obvious that you didn't settle for anything less than perfection. Isn't that right, Nicholas? May I call you Nicholas?" he asked, trying to appear polite.

Countess Boucher laughed. "I don't think Victor shall ever settle down."

Du Fay ignored her remark. "So, how long have you and Elena been in Paris?"

"A few months," I replied.

"And do you plan on leaving before the winter?"

"No," Elena answered. "Nicholas and I adore Paris. We are looking forward to spending Christmas here."

"Oh, that's good," the Countess interjected. "Victor holds the most lavish Christmas parties every year at his estate here in Versailles."

Just then the waiter arrived with my wine. "You don't drink Champagne?" Du Fay asked.

"No, just a little red wine," I answered. Something about Du Fay's polished smile was hard and untrustworthy. I tried to read his mind, but couldn't. The more he spoke, the more I disliked him. Resting my hand beside my glass, I noticed Du Fay staring at my ring. His expression changed.

"I hope you don't find me too inquisitive, but may I ask where you found such a unique ring?"

"It belonged to my father," I answered.

"Your father. Really?" Du Fay nodded, taking a puff on his cigar. His cool mannerism became slightly unsettled. "May I take a closer look?" he asked. "I have been trying to find a similar ring for a friend of mine."

Peering down over my hand, he stroked his thumb across the large ruby. His thin lips widened. "It certainly is a rare piece. Is your father still living?"

"No," I answered. His curious eyes glanced back at Elena, then back to me, clearly studying both of us. I began to feel something disturbingly cold about him as he sat quietly and glanced across the room.

His eyes switched back to me. "Katherine tells me you are a writer and that you prefer to work during the day. You're a brave man, Nicholas," he jested. "If I had a woman like Elena, I wouldn't want to let her out of my sight. You know all that writing indoors is not good for your health. You should get a little sun. You look so pale. Don't you agree, Elena?"

"No, not at all," she answered defensively.

Du Fay smiled at her reaction, but at the same time, there was something about his probing questions that made me suspicious. Again I tried to read him, while he continued to talk to another couple who stopped by to speak. Again, I couldn't channel into his thoughts. It was as if he was aware of what I was trying to do, as if his mind was challenging mine.

He turned around to put out his cigar and then glanced across the table at me with an evil glare. Whoever Du Fay was, or whatever he was trying to prove, it wasn't good. In fact, it felt dangerously bad. I didn't like the Countess, and I didn't like her friends, and after tonight, I wanted Elena to stay away from all of them. Catching her attention, I suggested we leave sooner than later. Elena agreed, and told Countess Boucher.

"Don't worry about me," the Countess said, her eyes glazed from all the champagne. "I shall travel back with Charles."

Du Fay overheard her. "Why are you leaving so soon?" he asked Elena. "The night is still young."

"Elena is tired, Victor," the Countess shouted.

He placed his drink on the table. "Then allow me to walk outside with you both. I need a little fresh air myself."

Not wanting to appear angry, I didn't reply. I didn't want to upset Elena. We were leaving. That was all that mattered.

Du Fay smirked arrogantly at me. "Come," he said, leading the way. "You should take Katherine's carriage. She won't need it now. She's traveling with Trembly."

Outside, Du Fay's eyes were fixed on Elena. "Did you enjoy tonight?" he asked, still trying to charm her. Just then, our carriage pulled up.

"My wrap," Elena called out, trying to catch it as it blew off her shoulders. Bending down to pick it up, I turned around and saw Elena holding Du Fay back as he made a pass to kiss her. Seething with anger, I pulled him away.

"What is wrong?" he said sarcastically. "Are you afraid you may lose her?"

"Wait in the carriage," I told Elena.

Before Du Fay could say anything more, I grabbed him by the collar, fighting to control the fire inside of me. He'd awakened my powers, and had now unlocked his own worse nightmare. My vampire eyes blazed into his eyes. "Understand one thing," I said. "This is no game Du Fay. You will not disrespect the woman I love. If you ever go near Elena again, I will destroy you."

He glared back at me as I let him go. He showed no fear. "I know what you are," he said, "and your threats do not scare me."

"If you know what I am," I answered, "then you will know to stay away if you value your life."

Du Fay stepped back, his face as hard as stone. "And if you understand what I am, Justine, then you would know to do the same."

Although I wanted to finish him, I pulled myself away. Elena was waiting. It was time to leave.

Back in the carriage, she was clearly nervous. "Nicholas, what happened out there?"

"Nothing," I answered, dropping my head so that she couldn't see my face.

"Nicholas? . . ."

"Please?" I said, trying to calm down. "Not now." I felt her fingers stroke the back of my head as I tried to hide the claw-like nails on my vampire hands.

"You don't have to hide anything from me," she whispered. "I love you, Nicholas. Please, let me hold your hand."

Tears of frustration filled my eyes as I let her take my unsightly hand. Tenderly, she kissed it and held it to her cheek. "My vampire, my love." The sound of her voice was like a calm blue ocean, a healing whisper that helped soothe my mind.

By the time we reached Paris, Elena was asleep. My woman, my angel, a child without judgment. She was going to be a mother, and I, a father. Our lives were about to change, and I vowed not to doubt myself. I was a vampire, but I knew how to love. Unlike my father, I wasn't about to turn away and avoid happiness because of my own fear.

Chapter Six

My Immortal Dilemma

For the next few days, I tried not to think about Du Fay's unsettling remarks. Though it played on my mind, I knew Elena hadn't visited the Countess since we'd left her at the ball. I'd asked her to keep her distance, and she'd promised me she'd do that. I never told her what had been said when I'd confronted Du Fay. It was my worry, not hers. Whatever he'd meant by saying he knew me, I was convinced he couldn't have known I was a vampire, or else he would have known not to question my power. What concerned me was that he'd seen me transform into something inhuman, and yet that didn't scare him. Why? I didn't know.

Though Elena never mentioned what she'd witnessed that night, I knew she was moved in a way that made her feel even more a part of my world. She began to ask questions about my immortality, questions I didn't fully understand myself. One night after we'd made love, she lay quiet, deep in thought. When I asked her what was wrong, I wished I hadn't.

I remember how she stared at me, how she looked into my eyes. "Nicholas," she said. "I know you don't like to talk about being a vampire, but there is something important I need to ask you. It's been playing on my mind ever since I found out I was pregnant."

"Tell me," I said, sensing her worry.

She paused. "Promise me you'll be honest, no matter how much the truth may upset me."

"I promise," I answered.

Not allowing me to look away, she gently held my face, as if she could read the truth in my eyes. "It's about your destiny, your immortality," she said. I want to know if what it says in that book is true. I read that all vampires stay young forever. Do you believe that's true, Nicholas?"

I'd dreaded the day Elena would ask me this. "I am not sure," I answered. "I do not know what is going to happen to me."

"You see," she said nervously, "that is what worries me. What will you do if you remain young when I am old? How would you feel? You wouldn't want me anymore. I would become a burden, an embarrassment to you."

"Stop, Elena. Don't think like this. Whatever happens, whether or not I remain young or get old, nothing will ever stop me from loving you. You are my life. Without you my life means nothing. Our child, our children, will love us for who we are, and they will always see how much I worship you. They will see the endless love I have for them and their mother."

Her tearful eyes looked away. "But when I die, you will continue to live on in this world. If you are immortal, then you will fall in love again and again. Our life together, our children, will become just a faded memory, a colorless dream. I don't want that to happen. I never want to leave you."

"Don't Elena. You're letting these thoughts and doubts take away what we have right now."

"Nicholas, don't you see what I am trying to say? I want to be with you forever. If you make me a vampire, make me immortal, then I will be able to share your immortal world."

What are you saying? Making you a vampire won't set us free. It's a curse, Elena. A sentence that one day would make you hate me. You don't understand the nightmare of having to survive on blood alone. Until you have had to drink the blood of animals, or even worse, another human being, you cannot imagine the hell and torment."

"But you do not drink human blood," she answered.

"That's right," I said, "but it doesn't stop my urge to do so. It's a continual fight, a fight not to become a monster, a murderer. Please Elena, I'm begging you to understand. I love you too much to ever make you a vampire. It doesn't matter to me that you will grow older. You are beautiful now, but you will always be beautiful. Today you are my princess, tomorrow you will be my queen. It's the fire in your soul that makes me love you so deeply."

"But one day you will forget me and begin again."

Holding her tenderly, I said, "Look at me. Read the love in my eyes. "If I am truly immortal, then I promise I will wait for your soul to come back to me. I will find you again, Elena. We will share a thousand lifetimes together. Ours will be an endless love affair that only dreams are made of."

I wiped her tears. "I hope you are right, Nicholas," she said.

I kissed her. "I know I am right."

That was the first time she had ever asked me to make her a vampire, and I knew in my heart it wouldn't be the last.

The next evening I found her searching the house for the ruby rose necklace I had given her the night of the ball. "I still haven't found it," she said desperately. "I asked the servants, and all of them said they haven't seen it. They've always been honest. I know I was wearing it when I left the ball. "It must have either dropped outside or in Katherine's carriage." Thinking out loud, she became more and more upset. "But if Katherine's driver had given it to her, surely she would have returned it by now. Oh, Nicholas, I can't bear to think I might have lost it."

I'd already told Elena I couldn't remember if she was wearing the necklace of not. I'd been so angry about Du Fay that I hadn't noticed it missing. Wanting her to try and forget about it, I suggested we go to the Carnival she had mentioned earlier that week.

"All right," she said, "but can we stop by Katherine's on the way? I need to ask her if she's heard anything about my necklace."

I agreed only because I didn't want Elena going there alone. As it turned out, the Countess was still in Versailles and wasn't due back for a couple of more days.

"Come," I told Elena. "Let's enjoy the night."

As we approached Montmartre, I saw Elena's eyes light up with excitement. Red and gold caravans lined the back streets of the area. Fire-eaters, magicians, and dancers entertained the crowd. Proud gypsy women stood outside beaded curtains enticing the curious to step inside and have their fortunes told. There was something wild and beautiful about some of the young gypsy women, their seductive manner, large fearless dark eyes, and long black hair thrown back off their bare shoulders. These women were strong, tireless travelers, their beauty as dangerous as a venomous snake. I found it intriguing, not just the attitude of the women, but of all the gypsy people. Their whole existence was one of letting go. These wayfarers had learned to survive and be free. They had a raw, magical energy that made one recognize the depth of our souls.

Suddenly, loud cheers, clapping, and singing turned our attention to the back of one of the caravans. On a small dirt path, a family of gypsies sat around an open fire. The smell of roasted pig filled the air as they cooked their supper on a large spit. They drank merrily beneath the black sky. One of the young men began playing his guitar.

We watched a couple get up and dance within the circle. Stomping their bare heels onto the ground, they clapped rhythmically to the hypnotic sounds. Such raw, natural talent was a treat to my eyes. Elena turned to me, loving every moment. I could see she felt connected to their energy and spirit. An old gray-haired man began to sing while raising his hands to his chest. He closed his eyes, lost in the music. His voice called out in waves of emotion like an Arabian sunrise across the gold desert sand. It was as if we'd stepped back in time and place. Captured by their unrehearsed performance, Elena and I watched, not wanting to leave. It wasn't until they stopped and began to eat that we realized how quickly an hour had passed.

Walking away, I heard a voice call out behind us. It was the old gypsy man who had been singing. He greeted us like a friend.

"Please, there is no need to leave," he shouted. "I noticed you enjoying the music. You are welcome to join us." He led us by the fire and made room for us on his blanket, which was neatly spread upon the ground. Placing a large jug of red wine and cups in front of us, he poured us some wine. "I am Juan, and this is my wife, Maria," he said, slicing some fruit on a large plate.

We learned they were from Andalucía and from a family of gypsies whose ancestry went back many generations. Suddenly, his wife Maria sat forward and asked Elena, "Have you had your fortune told?" Her large brown eyes stared playfully as she continued, "You love each other very much, and you are going to have many beautiful children together."

"Grandmamma," a young girl beside her interrupted, "why are you pretending to tell her fortune? You have to read her hand to see her future."

The old woman smiled. "My granddaughter is right."

"Are you going to tell her fortune, Grandmamma?" the young girl asked. "My Grandmamma is the greatest fortune teller in all the land. All the gypsies come to her. Don't they, Grandmamma?"

"Hush now," the old woman said lovingly. Taking her granddaughter's hand, she examined her palm. "Ah," she said. "I can see you are very tired, and it is your bedtime. Tomorrow will be busy. So you must rest and let the stars plan a new day." She smiled and hugged her goodnight. The little girl kissed her and ran into one of the caravans.

"Do you really read fortunes?" Elena asked.

"Yes." She nodded. "Would you like me to read yours?"

"Oh, would you?" Elena said, sitting forward.

"Of course," she answered.

"We are happy to pay you," I said.

She shook her head. "I do not charge family, and tonight you are a part of our family. Please, it is my gift to you. Let's go inside."

We followed her and her husband into their caravan. She asked us to sit at a small table, where she lit a lamp.

"Before I begin, I must know if you want me to tell you everything that appears in your hand," she said in the voice of a mother warning a child. "I will not lie to you, but if you choose, I will avoid anything to do with death or illness."

"Please, I want to know everything," Elena told her.

"Very well." She smiled. "Extend your right palm."

The old gypsy closed her eyes and inhaled deeply as if she were asking a higher force to help her. Slowly she exhaled and opened her eyes. Her fingers ran down and across the lines on Elena's palm as if she were scrutinizing a faded map. "I can see you have felt very unhappy in the past. I see an older man. Your father, but he has disappointed you. There has been confusion and unrest." Again, she stared back into her palm. "Something happened. Something about a marriage."

Elena nodded. "Yes."

"You chose to follow your heart, take a different path." The gypsy looked up and watched Elena's nervous smile. "Do not worry," she said, "You chose wisely."

A moment passed, and the old woman continued. "I feel you've been trying to reach out to someone overseas. I see letters you have written, letters to your father. You have not yet received an answer. Try not to worry. There is still anger and confusion concerning your decision. Your mother is happy for you." She smiled quietly. "She admires your strength."

"What about my father?" Elena asked.

"He does love you, but his pride stands in the way. It will take time for him to accept what has happened. You have traveled far to find happiness, and a lot of love surrounds you at this moment. There is no doubt how much your partner loves you. His adoration and respect shine out in your hand. Also, there is joyful news, a child."

"Yes," Elena said, beaming. "I am with child."

The old gypsy smiled kindly, then suddenly her eyes widened. Her expression was one of concern. "Wait," she said. "I see someone watching." Her worried tone became more and more anxious. "There is a man," she said, "a dark stranger. You must beware. He hides in the shadows of the night. Heavy clouds are moving fast. This is a warning, a sign of change. Whoever this stranger is, his intentions are bad. He wants to make trouble. You may not have met him yet, but mark my words, you will. I cannot see his face or hear his name, but I feel his power. He demands and controls everything around him. He is wicked, an evil man." Her mouth tightened. "You mustn't trust him. You and Nicholas must never trust him."

Immediately I thought about Victor Du Fay as Elena panicked and asked, "Why would this man want to harm us?"

"I do not know." The gypsy shook her head. "I cannot see the answer. All I know is that you must beware."

Seeing Elena becoming more and more anxious, I said, "Maybe you should stop the reading."

The gypsy didn't listen to me. She was too intent on trying to see an answer. "I don't understand this." She frowned. "Do you have a brother here or another young man living with you?"

"No," Elena answered.

She looked up at her. "That's strange. Is there someone else close to you who is troubled? A man suffers deeply. He cannot sleep. He walks the night. Maybe he is ill and is trying to hide it. There is blood on his pillow, but I cannot see his face. Do you know who I am talking about? Whoever it is, he loves you dearly."

Elena shook her head. "No," she said uneasily, as if realizing the gypsy was talking about me. Before Elena had a chance to pull her hand away, the gypsy pointed her finger into Elena's palm.

"There," she called out. "Again, I see the same evil shadow, the same dark stranger. His presence is becoming stronger. Dear God," she said, making the sign of the cross. "It is almost as if he is watching all of us. He knows you are here."

Suddenly, she began to cough uncontrollably. Her husband fetched some water.

"Maria, are you all right?" he asked her, holding her as she tried to drink."

"Yes," she gasped, slowly looking as if she'd recovered.

Her husband stood up and walked us outside, assuring us his wife would be fine. "I am sorry if Maria scared you," he said. "I have never seen her react like that before."

Thanking him again for their hospitality, we said goodnight. Shaken by the old gypsy's reaction, Elena grabbed my arm. I convinced her not to worry, but I knew that tomorrow I would have to explain my concerns about Count Victor Du Fay.

That night I decided not to leave Elena alone. I drank the blood of rats in the cellar. The gypsy's warning played on my mind.

I was Elena's vampire, her lover, her protector. When I left her sleeping, I needed to know she was safe. This was our nocturnal world, an incomprehensible reality, a vision of confusion in a gypsy's eyes

Back in my study, while Elena slept, I watched the logs crackle on a welcome fire as my thoughts drifted back to my childhood. Knowing I was going to be a father made me think about my mother, my life, my innocence, and how I'd wished I'd known her. Being rejected and ignored growing up had laid a heavy blanket of doubt around my shoulders. Every time I felt happy or fulfilled, I would feel that same blanket of uncertainty wrap itself around me, awakening the painful memories of my father. The scars of his silence had never gone away. I remembered as a young child wandering down the dark long corridors in the middle of the night to my mother's old room.

Ever since the day she had passed away, my father had insisted her room remain locked. It became a mystery to me, a child's silent hope that maybe somehow she could still be alive. I remember thinking that if I could only step inside her room, I might find her sitting on her bed smiling at me, her arms open waiting to embrace her only son. It was sad, too sad for words. I imagined that every shadow passing across my bedroom wall was my mother trying to reach out to me. I believed her spirit was sending me a sign, telling me she loved me through the moonlit shadows on my wall. I became a desperate little boy, waiting night after night down the forgotten hallway outside my mother's room. I'd sit on the floor, holding my candle until my bare feet became so cold that I'd have no other choice but to return to my bed. So many times, I would stare up at her portrait in the drawing room and watch her eyes watching over me. If I looked long enough, I could see her chest breathing, her hands moving as she smiled down upon me.

My mother was alive, I would tell myself. But then, like everything else in life, one day you realize the cruel reality, that it was a desperate dream, a child's fantasy. I thanked God for Charlotte, the only person I felt truly loved me. It wasn't until I was around 10 years old that I accepted my mother's death. But still my troubled mind couldn't rest while I slept. I never dared tell my father about my sleepwalking, and Charlotte didn't either. She just tried to comfort me as a mother comforts a son.

Even in my early teens, I began to have the same recurring nightmare. It was so intense and frightening that I can still remember it to this day. I'd find myself in the middle of an endless black sea where hooded, gray spirits walked across the hellish black water. The faceless spirits would wave their arms, beckoning me to follow them. My terror of being left alone in the darkness petrified me. Grabbing one of their ghostly white hands, I believed they were there to save me. Suddenly the deafening cries of the hooded spirits would begin to echo and call out my name as one by one they began to drown. My panic of dying made my body begin to sink into the water as I watched a towering black wave rise over me. Just before it hit me, I'd be thrown back in my bed to the lightning and unforgiving sound of thunder outside my bedroom window.

The window would fly open crashing against the wall sending my papers and books hurling into the air. Trying to fight the storm, I'd throw myself toward the window to close it. But as I would grab the lock, a terrifying face would appear at the window. Its chalk-white skin and blood-red eyes would fly toward me. Trying to escape, I would feel my nails scraping at the locked door until my fingers bled. I tried to yell. I wanted to run, but my body was frozen, unable to move. That was when I'd wake up, drenched in sweat, shaking with shock. The nightmare would be over, but my fear remained.

It wasn't until my father died that I felt a sense of relief. I had wanted to love him so much, but the pain of that desperation had been too much to bear. Since I had become a vampire, something had drawn me closer to his memory. The fact that I had made such a terrible mistake and had to face my eternal curse had helped me see and understand that my father was only human. Although he had treated me cruelly, surviving my childhood and all its demons had helped me survive the torment of what I had become. I knew it was time to try and cleanse myself of all the dark memories that still haunted me. Elena's pregnancy was another chance to make matters right. I wanted to believe my father had really loved me. Now more than ever, it was important for me to forgive him.

I stared across at the empty red leather chair in front of me. It reminded me of the one my father kept in his study. I could still see him reading his paper, his presence always dominating the room. He constantly carried an intense energy that was scary and dark. When he chose to look at me, I could feel him scanning my thoughts, making me feel vulnerable and weak. Maybe it was an old trick he had used that helped him become such a feared solicitor. I don't know, but the one thing I was certain of was, it had made me feel like an open book.

I poured myself some wine and tried to bring myself back to the present. Taking out my diary, I continued to make notes about my journey as a vampire. I felt an odd cool breeze drift through the room, moving the drapes as it passed. Was it my imagination, or had the lights suddenly dimmed? The steady, long flames from the candelabras were burning unnaturally low. The room had suddenly become icy cold, so cold the hairs on my arms rose with its eerie chill. I checked the windows. None of them was open, and the door was still closed. A terrible smell of decay lingered in the air, and I began to sense an evil presence. Whatever it was, I could feel its uncomfortable aura swirling silently around me. This was not a friendly encounter, and now I could see a smoky gray mist rising from the corner of the room.

The ghostly vision was beginning to take shape. Its human form was transparent. The outline of its body had a thin, silvery glow that stretched towards the high ceiling. I sought to move closer but could not. My limbs had stiffened. My muscles had tightened. I was motionless. All I could do was try to will it away. Whatever it was, it was forcing its darkness upon me. I could feel it circling the room as if it were getting ready to strike. Still I could not move.

Through the ghostly gray smoke, I suddenly saw a demonic face. Its beaming white eyes glared out from the dark corner. My head began to thud and pound while my heart raced. Suddenly the silvery figure began to fade. Watching it disappear, my body was released from its spell. Turning around frantically, I ran upstairs to check on Elena, relieved to see she was still asleep, breathing calmly.

I became worried and shaken by what had just happened. I raced back to my study. Something dangerous had just entered our home, and I had no idea where it had come from or what it was. Trying not to panic, I thought about Du Fay. I remembered what he had said that night before leaving the ball. I remembered his eyes glaring back at me, unafraid when I'd warned him. That ghostly figure that had just departed now left me whispering his name.

Du Fay's words began to echo back to me. "And if you know who I am, Justine, you will know to do the same. *And if you know who I am Justine, you will know to do the same.*"

He had witnessed my face change, seen my eyes become pools of blood. He felt the presence of a vampire but showed no fear. I began to wonder. Could I have been looking into the eyes of another vampire? I knew then I had to see him again. I had to find out who or what Count Victor Du Fay truly was.

A WALK IN THE SUN

The old gypsy women had read the signs of danger in Elena's hand. But that didn't scare me. I was a vampire. Danger had become the map of my survival. It would soon be daybreak, and tonight I thought, tonight at sunset, I would find Du Fay.

CHAPTER SEVEN

THE DEVIL'S CALLING

*A*s the morning sun melted like butter across the foot of Elena's bed, I could never have imagined what was going to occur that day. I had told her not to worry about the old gypsy's warning, and as always, Elena trusted me. If I had known or even half understood the unimaginable evil that was about to occur, I would have taken her somewhere safe until I knew she was free of danger. Last night when I'd rushed upstairs to check on her, little did I know that would be the last time I would see Elena sleeping.

The following morning she awoke, glad to welcome a new day. She tried not to think about what the gypsy had told her and stepped out onto her terrace inhaling the wonderful smell of the damp chestnut trees. Though the gray clouds threatened a morning shower, she enjoyed the drop of rain that brushed her nose. Downstairs in the drawing room, she had breakfast by the fire and read the morning paper.

The housekeeper knocked quietly. "Excuse me, Madame. I am sorry to disturb you, but Countess Boucher is here to see you."

Elena placed her cup and saucer on the table. "Show her in," she said, smiling. "And please bring some fresh tea and pastries."

No sooner had the young maid left than Elena could hear the Countess shuffling and complaining down the hall. She waddled into the drawing room, cheerfully loud. "Good morning, my dear," she bellowed, her plump round cheeks flushed from the brisk morning breeze. "I hope I'm not disturbing you. I arrived back from Versailles late last night and couldn't wait to see you. James told me you and Nicholas had called at the house yesterday?"

"Of course you are not disturbing me," Elena assured her. "It is good to know you are back safe and sound."

The Countess grinned, plopping herself down in front of the fire. As she began adjusting the cushions behind her back to make more space to settle her large behind, the maid entered with some fresh tea and pastries.

"Oh what a good idea." She grinned. "There is nothing like tea and cake to accompany a healthy gossip." Digging into a chocolate éclair, she looked across at Elena. "So, my dear, I haven't had a chance to ask you. Did you enjoy the royal ball? I know you were tired but I do hope you had a good time."

Elena immediately thought about her necklace. "Yes, thank you. I had a wonderful time." Waiting until the Countess finished her pastry, she said, "I seem to have lost my ruby rose necklace. Have you heard anything about it?"

"Your necklace? Of course," the Countess said. "I have good news. You're a lucky girl, Elena. Victor found it outside on the driveway when you left the ball. He left it for me to pick up at his house."

Elena breathed a sigh of relief. "Do you mean Count Du Fay?"

"Yes, of course," she said with a nod. "Didn't he walk outside with you and Nicholas?"

"Yes," Elena answered, remembering the trouble that night.

"I do have a small confession," the Countess said. "That is why I am here so early. Unfortunately, I forgot to collect it. I thought we could pick it up today if you like."

Elena's heart dropped as she tried not to appear disappointed. "But you only arrived back last night," she said. "You must be tired. I couldn't ask you to do that for me."

"Oh don't be silly," the Countess said. "I forgot to pick it up, and now I'm worried because Victor left for Cornwall yesterday, so your necklace may not be safe. I don't trust those young maids. They'll steal anything."

"But wouldn't the Count know to put it into his safe?"

"Yes, I suppose." She shrugged. "But I told you Victor left for Cornwall yesterday. He may not have remembered to do that. I really think it's best we collect your necklace today." Taking a sip of tea, she smiled. "Why don't you ask Nicholas if he would like to join us?"

Elena paused knowing that was not possible. "What about tonight? We could go there tonight."

"Elena," the Countess said, "this morning I can go there with you, but tonight would be too tiring for me.

"Of course, I'm sorry," Elena said. "It is just, well, Nicholas left early this morning to attend to some business. He won't be back until this evening."

"Then leave him a note, child," the Countess suggested. "We'll be back before sunset."

Elena thought for a moment. She wanted her necklace more than anything, and she didn't want to chance it being stolen. Count Du Fay had left for Cornwall. It didn't seem to matter if she collected it today. "All right." She stood up. "Give me a moment to change, and we'll leave."

"I'll wait here," the Countess answered, pouring herself some more tea.

Elena went upstairs and changed. Taking a piece of paper from her drawer, she went downstairs and asked for the Count's address. Madame Boucher gave her the address, watching her closely as she wrote her message for Nicholas and placed it on the mantel.

The Countess smiled. "Are we ready now? We'll take my carriage." Elena grabbed her shawl, and together they left the room. Suddenly Elena turned around and went back into the drawing room. "What are you doing?" the Countess asked.

Elena took a red rose from the vase on the table and placed it next to her note. "Now I am ready," she said. As they walked out into the drizzly air, Elena stepped into the carriage.

The Countess stopped. "Oh dear," she exclaimed. "I think I must have dropped one of my earrings in the drawing room."

Elena sat forward. "I will go back and check for you."

"No, don't be silly," the Countess insisted. "You stay there. I'll go back and take a quick look. It's probably on the chair."

Elena waited as the Countess walked back inside the house and rushed into the drawing room. Her evil hands snatched Elena's note. Then viciously, she crumpled it up in her hands. Calmly, she went outside and quickly threw it over the rails of the steps.

Elena turned and smiled unknowingly as the Countess Boucher climbed into the carriage. "Did you find your earring?" Elena asked.

"Yes, it was by the chair," she answered.

As the carriage pulled away under the gloomy, dull sky, Elena's note lay amongst the damp autumn leaves.

Side by side they passed through the streets, leading west out of the city. The Countess smiled smugly. "It looks like a storm may be on its way."

Elena looked up at the heavy, dark clouds moving fast across the troubled sky. She remembered what the gypsy had told her. Maybe this wasn't such a good idea after all, or was she just being too superstitious? As they progressed away from the city, a faint mist hung over the trees of the surrounding countryside. Elena checked her watch. They'd been traveling well over an hour. "Is it much farther, Katherine?" she asked, beginning to feel a little uneasy.

"No," the Countess replied. "I told you Victor lives in Versailles. We should be there within another hour or so." She patted Elena's knee reassuringly. "You shouldn't worry so much, child."

Elena sat back. She trusted the Countess. She shouldn't worry. She knew that if the weather proved bad she had left Nicholas a note with Count Du Fay's address.

Another hour passed. Then suddenly the driver veered off the main path. They were now heading down a muddy path through the woods. As the carriage bumped and rocked, Elena held on to her seat. "Does the driver know where he's going?"

The Countess smiled confidently. "Yes, he has brought me here many times before. We are almost there."

All at once, the coach began to slow down. They had shifted out of the woods. "Here we are," the Countess said sharply. Elena looked straight ahead at the two towering black iron gates and the huge stone walls that surrounded the grounds. It looked more like a fortress than a mansion. An eerie stillness hung in the air. Everything about it signified restriction.

"Isn't it marvelous?" the Countess said, her voice filled with admiration.

Elena said nothing as she continued to watch the black oppressive gates begin to creak open. Entering down the graveled path, she looked around the gray, colorless grounds. There were no flowers. No pretty ponds or benches. Nothing warm or inviting to be seen. Only gray ugly stone gargoyles that stared across the neatly cut lawn. Even the well-groomed trees seemed hauntingly still against the dark heavy clouds. As they approached the house, she couldn't help but feel a dark, foreboding energy. She felt she was being watched, as if every window of the cold, creepy mansion seemed to be staring down with a ghostlike presence. The driver climbed down and opened the carriage door. Elena sat still clutching her purse nervously.

"Well," the Countess said, standing outside. "Aren't you getting out?"

Elena nodded and stepped out onto the damp gravel. Then they traversed up the stone steps to the great black doors, where a beady-eyed butler greeted them and showed them inside the eerie entrance, past the heavy gold mirrors and a large portrait of the Count. The butler led them into the drawing room.

"The Count will join you shortly," he announced.

Elena turned to the Countess. "I thought you said Count Du Fay had left for Cornwall?"

"Oh, stop whining," the Countess said impatiently. "A little mistake. What does it matter?"

Elena noticed Katherine's unfriendly tone and sat down quietly, confused by her sharpness. She stared around at the suggestive objects and lavish furnishings. The heavy velvet black-and-gold drapes, the unusual tapestries hung on the walls, the tall crimson leather chairs and long red sofa that made one feel they had entered some dark and secret room. Two immense stone lions roared from each side of the huge, impressive fireplace. She didn't want to be there, but it was too late. She stared up at the provocative nude portrait of a young woman above the fireplace. Her bewitching green eyes looked down like glistening jewels over the long flames from the fire, almost pulling one into the picture.

Everything about Du Fay's taste and preference appeared to be vulgar and dark. It ignited the imagination with desire and sin that demanded attention. It was horribly overbearing.

Suddenly the door opened, and Count Du Fay entered. His commanding presence unnerved Elena as he walked over to her and kissed her hand.

"How wonderful it is to see you again, Elena," he said. Turning to the Countess, he greeted her warmly. "And of course it is always a pleasure to see you, Katherine." Elena tried not to appear worried, but still she found it difficult to hide her nervousness. He sat opposite Elena, his strong, dark gaze fixed upon her beauty. "So, how was your journey?"

"It was fine, thank you." Elena replied, trying not to appear uncomfortable.

The short, cagey-eyed butler walked in carrying three glasses of champagne and some hors d'oeuvres on a silver tray. He sat them on the table. "Will there be anything else?" he asked.

Elena sat forward, "May I have a glass of water?"

The Count smiled. "Of course," He stood and picked up two glasses of champagne, offering one to Elena. "Isn't this meant to be a celebration? After all, I did find your necklace."

Elena nodded shyly, "Yes, I was so relieved when Katherine told me."

The Count sat back and sipped his champagne. "It certainly is a charming piece. Quite different."

"Yes," Elena answered softly. "It was a gift from Nicholas."

Du Fay's eyes widened. "How is Nicholas?" Is he still annoyed with me for finding you irresistibly beautiful?"

Elena didn't like Du Fay's forward remark. "Actually, Nicholas hasn't mentioned anything about you since that night."

"I'm glad he decided to take my advice."

Elena didn't understand what Du Fay meant by his remark, but thought it best not to ask. Countess Boucher stood up, "Victor, would you excuse me? I feel I need a little fresh air."

"Should I come with you?" Elena asked, not wanting to be left alone.

"No, you stay here. I won't be long."

Du Fay watched her leave the room. Sensing Elena was eager to leave, he switched the conversation. "Tell me, do you like horses?"

"Yes," she said nervously.

"Come, follow me," he said. Leading her out the house, he walked her across the courtyard to his stables. Playfully, he introduced her to his handsome, black stallion. "This is Prince, a true champion. Would you care to ride him? I'll take one of the other horses. What do you say?" Before she had a chance to answer, a sudden flash of lightening thundered across the heavy, gray sky. All at once, it began to pour. "Well, maybe next time," he said graciously. Taking Elena's hand, he said, "We'd better hurry."

Once inside, Du Fay stared as he watched her pat her dress dry by the fire. He was desperate to have her. She looked even more ravishing with her hair and face wet from the rain. Wanting to hold her, kiss her, and lick the drops of rain from her neck and bosom, he waited quietly and sipped his drink. He had been searching for a woman like Elena, someone who could be his queen, his temptress. She had the face of an angel, with a body made for sin.

Beneath her innocence, she was smart and mystifying, and he knew Elena could keep a secret. The fact that she'd chosen to love a vampire convinced him she was willing to accept anything the devil might ask of her. His lustful eyes continued to undress her until he saw Elena catch him staring.

Discretely, she lifted her hand over her bosom. "Where is Katherine? Shouldn't she be back by now?"

Du Fay finished the rest of his champagne. "I'll check on her," he said. As he left the room, Elena looked at her watch. It was getting close to four o'clock, and all she could think about was the note she had left for Nicholas. If she didn't get back soon, she assumed he would come find her. Feeling nervous and vulnerable, she wanted to get away. If she didn't leave soon, she feared the worst. She knew how angry Nicholas would be when he discovered she'd left and gone to Du Fay's home. Just then Du Fay returned, holding her necklace. "Katherine is fine," he said. "She's taking a nap in the study. Here is your necklace."

Elena was relieved and hoped that soon they'd be leaving. Without asking, Du Fay placed it around her neck.

"Let me fasten it for you." He brushed her hair off her shoulders and then he tried to kiss her.

Elena jumped back, "What are you doing?"

Du Fay stared into her eyes. "Come now, Elena. You know how much I am attracted to you."

Removing his hand off her shoulder, Elena tried not to offend him. "I am sorry if you've misjudged me, Mr. Du Fay, but I didn't come here for this. I only came here to collect my necklace. If I'd have known you were home, I wouldn't have come at all."

"I don't believe you," Du Fay said. "I know you like me. You just don't want to accept it."

"Please, Mr. Du Fay. You know I love Nicholas. If I have given you the wrong impression, I'm truly sorry."

Du Fay listened to her, undisturbed by her reaction. Quietly, he asked, "What would you say if I told you I believe you are the one I have been waiting to share my life with? When I first laid eyes on you at the ball, I knew we were meant for each other."

"No. You're wrong. You're making a mistake," Elena said. "Nicholas is the only one I love. Please, you have to understand."

"I do understand," he answered. "I understand that you believe you are in love when really you are not. I know you came to Paris to escape being married to a man you did not love. Trust me. Nicholas is not right for you. He doesn't deserve you. He cannot love you the way I would love you. I can offer you the world, Elena. Anything your heart desires, I can give you. I have the power to grant whatever you wish. There is nothing I cannot do."

Elena moved back, afraid of Du Fay's unbalanced response. She wanted to get away, run out of the house, but there was nowhere to run. She felt trapped. Again, he tried to kiss her.

"Please." She felt a wave of panic. "I don't want to be with you. I have told you I love Nicholas. Nothing you say will change that."

His expression hardened. He got up and walked to the window, trying to control his frustration. Turning around, his ruthless eyes stared back at her coolly. "You think I don't know the dark secret you hide, don't you, Elena? You think I don't know that you have chosen to be with a vampire."

Her heart raced with fear. " I don't know what you are ..."

"Stop," Du Fay commanded. "Do not insult my adept intelligence. I can see through your lies. My powers are above and beyond anything you can imagine. Please allow me to enlighten you." He smiled wickedly. "I am a master of the sacred arts. You may have witnessed the feeble powers of your vampire, but believe me, whatever you have seen cannot compare to my strength and magic. Why do you think your precious Nicholas has not mentioned our conversation that night at the ball? You saw his face. You witnessed his reaction when he got in the carriage. Well, I will tell you why Elena. Because he is afraid. He knows I recognized what he was. He knew that night he couldn't defeat me. He doesn't love you Elena. A bloodthirsty beast like that doesn't know how to love. "

"You have no right to say that," she cried out. "You know nothing about Nicholas. All you talk about is power. I don't care how powerful you are. I don't care about your opinion. I love Nicholas."

He laughed as if amused. "I am sorry if the truth hurts, but isn't it time you raised your head out of the sand? Nicholas Justine is nothing more than a hideous mistake, a freak of nature that serves no purpose. Vampires belong in freak shows, not with beautiful women like you."

Bursting into tears, Elena couldn't take any more. Running for the door, she tried to leave. Du Fay leapt across the room, his eyes ablaze with arrogance. Grabbing her, he kicked the door shut and pressed her up against it.

"You're going nowhere," he said. "Not until I'm finished."

"Please let me go. You can't do this. Let me go," Elena cried.

The more Du Fay watched her struggle, the more aroused he became. Forcing himself upon her, he ripped open the front of her dress grabbing her breasts wildly. Tears fell down her cheeks as he slammed her arms up against the door and threatened to beat her if she tried to move. Turning her head towards the window, she bit her lip terrified to fight back.

As the rain cried down the long panes of glass, Elena wept silently, too scared to move. Du Fay continued to enjoy the moment, licking and kissing her naked flesh. Releasing her arms, he pulled up her dress. It was then Elena noticed the heavy gold candle holder on the table beside the door. Quickly she grabbed it and swung out with all her might, striking Du Fay on the side of his head.

He fell back onto the floor. Running out into the hallway, Elena screamed out for help. She rushed into the study to find Madame Boucher only to discover she had left. The front doors were locked. There was no one around, no butler, no servants, no one to help her. Crying hysterically, she scrambled down the hallway past the oval staircase to what looked like another side entrance of the house. Again, she realized there was no escape. The door had been bolted from the outside. At that moment, she heard Du Fay's voice loudly bellowing down the hall after her. Petrified, she removed her shoes and ran down the nearest corridor looking for a place to hide. Du Fay's sadistic roar echoed around the unforgiving walls.

"There's no way out." His wicked laugh chilled her. "You can't hide from me!" His psychopathic tone shook her body with so much terror she thought she might pass out.

"Oh God, please help me," she wept. "Please!" Feeling lost in the maze of corridors, she suddenly noticed a small trap door in the floor. Pulling it open, she stepped inside, managing to pull the door closed above her head. Shaking with terror, she descended down the crooked stone steps into what appeared to be a lighted cellar.

Through a haze of tears, she stared up at the lit iron torches hanging from the low, damp rotting beams across the cellar. A large rat scurried from beneath the stairs and disappeared into the darkness. Fear and desperation raced through her body. In less than twelve hours, her world had become a living hell. It was as if she were locked in some macabre nightmare unable to move, unable to escape. Feeling her heart pounding with fright, she heard a shuffling of chains, followed by a faint moan. Too scared to call out, she heard it again—a faint gasping moan that sounded like a woman's voice. Picking up a lit torch that had been left just off the floor, she tried to see who was there. Moving forward, she was overwhelmed by a foul odor hanging in the air, an odor so bad it made her want to vomit. Her eyes caught sight of blood-stained walls, and her mind began to race with fear and dread. She heard a woman's cry a few feet away. Turning around, she raised her torch, aghast at what Du Fay had done. Lying chained in a corner, she saw a naked girl, her beaten body left freezing on the soiled, damp stone floor. Her long tangled black hair draped over her bruised face. Frantic to help her, Elena tried to lift her up against the wall. "It's all right. I won't hurt you. I am going to fetch help," she whispered.

The girl moaned out in agony as her back touched the wall. Elena gasped, noticing the deep cuts from a lashing on her back. Laying her down on her side, Elena removed the petticoat from beneath her dress and covered her legs. Tears of terror filled Elena's eyes. She couldn't leave the cellar, not yet. Du Fay was a monster, a sadistic evil psychopath. She would have to go back into the house. There was no other way out.

Just then, the cellar door crashed open. "I know you are in here," Du Fay yelled furiously. Charging down into the cellar, his face roared with anger as he found Elena standing by the tortured girl. He glared unmercifully down at the ravaged girl, then looked at Elena, seething with rage. "You should never have come down here. Do you realize what you have done? You have ruined everything. Your heart will never rise to tell what you have witnessed here today.

He pounced toward her and swiped his hand across her face. Blood gushed through Elena's fingers as she lay now, trembling on the floor, holding her cheek. Again, Du Fay screamed at her. "Do you understand what you have done?" He kicked her viciously.

Unable to answer, Elena nodded as she crouched beneath him, sobbing helplessly.

"Good," Du Fay answered, "Because now I am going to have to kill you." Dragging her by the hair, he began pulling her across the floor towards the steps. Elena begged for mercy, screaming out hysterically. Ignoring her screams, Du Fay grabbed her arms and began dragging her face down up the stone steps. Wanting to disfigure her, he dragged her up the steps allowing her face to slam into the rough hard stone. Out of the cellar, he proceeded down the hall, pulling her like a rag-doll back into the drawing room, and dropping her on the floor.

Then he sat and stared like the devil at her bloodied face. "What a pity it is to see such beauty destroyed. I wonder what your vampire would think of you now."

Elena could hardly move, as she tried to remain conscious.

Du Fay leaned back in his chair, continuing to reveal his sadistic inhuman soul. "Let me ask you something, Elena? Was being faithful to your vampire really worth all this pain? I offered you the world, and you denied me. I dare say, your unquestionable loyalty deserves applause, but where is your vampire now? Is he on his way here to save you? I don't think so." He began pacing the room, enjoying his own voice as he played with his victim. "You see my sweet," he said, "I have a different opinion about life's devotion and loyalty. I believe it to be one of man's greatest weaknesses. It is a misinterpretation of the truth. Deluding oneself by allowing guilt to drive one's soul is beyond ridiculous." He turned and glanced at Elena, ignoring her suffering, as if nothing had happened.

He continued ranting madly, "Only a coward avoids what he truly desires. I see it all the time. Men choose to be loyal to their wives, their church, their profession, all because of guilt and fear. Why do they do this? The answer is obvious. Because they are afraid, afraid of God, afraid of the devil. It's quite hilarious when you think about it," he said pouring himself a cognac. "Please forgive me for not offering you a brandy, but I think it may sting that tear on your lip."

Elena didn't answer. She didn't dare move. She daren't look away. Her only hope was that Nicholas had found the note she had left for him and that he was on his way to find her. Her swollen bruised eyes watched Du Fay continue to preach as he paced the room.

Sitting back down, he paused for a moment and looked at her, as he sipped his brandy. "You are probably wondering why I am bothering to talk to you," he said. "Maybe it is because I still feel drawn to you. It's as if we have known each other before. You almost make me want to let you live, but unfortunately I cannot allow that. You must know by now that I didn't plan this to happen. I am not the monster, Elena. My work, my passion, is to unlock the prison of man's conscience. My powers are not evil. They merely hold up the mirror that reflects the truth. I am a black magician. I help people recognize who they really are, who they want to be without guilt or judgment. Sometimes, human sacrifice is necessary. That girl you saw in the cellar was nothing more than a common prostitute. I didn't force her to come here. She came of her own free will. Her greed sealed her fate."

He paused to finish his brandy. "Her soul is worth much more to me than it is to her. Some humans are like vermin. They have nothing to offer except disease and ignorance.

But the soul! Now that has a great many uses. When you chose to love a vampire, you made a terrible mistake. Vampires belong to a lost world. They are bothersome, useless creatures that serve no purpose. Your vampire is no different than any other. He does not care about you. He cannot feel love. Didn't you leave him a note? He knows where you are, and he knows my reasons for bringing you here." He grinned. "He is too afraid to come for you."

Trying not to listen to Du Fay's evil remarks, Elena dropped her head and prayed for strength. Suddenly, Du Fay sensed her prayers disrupting his sadistic mind. Leaping from his chair, his eyes glazed with fury. He pushed his fist into her bloodied face.

"How dare you utter the words of God in my presence? Does this look like a church to you? Does anything here suggest your futile savior is welcome here?" Grabbing her by the hair, he lifted her face up toward the window. "Look out there, he demanded. "The sun has gone down, the night has begun. Where is your God? Where is your vampire? There is no one to hear your prayers, no one." He dropped her.

Unable to listen to Du Fay's torturous words any longer, Elena cried out. "You can kill me and my unborn child, but you'll never destroy my soul or my love for Nicholas. None of your powers can change that. Nicholas and I will share lifetimes to come, and this day, this moment will be forgotten forever."

Shaking with fury, Du Fay turned slowly, revealing the demons within his distorted face. Like a growling beast, he answered her, "If you love your vampire so much, then it is only right that you and your unborn child should die a vampire's death!" Pulling her up, he threw her onto the hearth, pressing his foot into her stomach. Gasping for breath, Elena struggled, but nothing could stop Du Fay now. Grabbing the silver poker, he ignored her cries, as he grasped it with both hands, and pointed it down above her chest. "Let this be a lesson to haunt your soul forever."

He drove the poker through her heart. All at once Elena's screams were replaced by silence. Du Fay stared down at her dead body, his face and hands stained with her blood.

A storm of demons filled his eyes as thunder and lightening shook the windows. Snatching the ruby necklace off her neck, he snarled like a beast ready for war.

"Let's see what your vampire does now," he growled, and spat.

That night he drove Elena's bloody corpse back to Paris and deposited her body on the muddy cobbles of a deserted alley near the Champs D'Elysee. Like a black hooded ghost protected by the devil, he returned to Versailles without remorse or regret. His plans remained intact. Tomorrow his ritual of death would take place. The girl in the cellar would be sacrificed. Then he and his disciples would leave for Cornwall. Everything was arranged. There would be no delays.

Back in the house, Du Fay sat and pondered how long it would take before Nicholas discovered that it was he who had murdered Elena. He envisioned the next time they would meet face to face. "Soon Justine," he uttered "Soon you will know that I am the Master."

CHAPTER EIGHT

COUNT VICTOR DU FAY

And Jesus asked,
"For what does it profit a man to gain the whole world
and yet suffer the loss of his own soul?"
The black magician replied, "Everything."

Do not ask why, after you have received.
Do not beg forgiveness after you have indulged.
I am the artist that portrays your desires.
Your mind is my canvas; now tell me your pleasure.
The decadence of sin surrounds all you will
Be careful what you wish for; I am here to grant it.
For I am the master of the infernal black arts
An adept of the formidable left hand path
I am the demon you dread in all your nightmares

Your soul is mine to use as I will.
Dare to defy me; you will die without mercy.
I will crucify your soul on the cross of your savior
Your Christ will not save you; there will be no remorse
For I will hang your heart from the thorns of his crown
I am Count Victor Du Fay
I am a black magician.

Victor Du Fay

A forgotten old church deep inside the woods had proved to be the perfect location for the devil's ceremony. Du Fay stood waiting for his disciples to bring him the girl. His black hooded cloak bore the marks of the Pentagram. Long black candles lit the Satanic table. A chalice was placed beneath the table; his alter of death was ready. Du Fay placed the silver dagger on the stone pedestal and stared down at his hooded disciples, his wicked eyes glazed in the moment. Tonight, the bloody sacrifice would evoke the dark angel of destruction. Its beastly head would soon rise from its grave to serve Du Fay's demands.

Among the shadowed faces, stood Countess Boucher. Her appearance no longer revealed that of a harmless old woman. No. Instead, her cold, callous stare demanded that the devil's work must be done. A true apprentice of the left hand path, she was proud to be one of Du Fay's most loyal servants.

The faint sound of cries and heavy chains broke the still night air outside. The doors of the abandoned chapel swung open. Ignoring the whispers of excitement in the room, Du Fay's eyes watched intently as his victim was dragged toward the alter. He stood composed like a king as she pleaded to be spared, and was thrown down at his feet. Her tangled, long hair fell over her bruised face. She was the same girl Elena had found in Du Fay's cellar, kept prisoner for over two weeks, her body chained to the walls of a living hell.

"Please don't kill me," she sobbed. "Please." Her muddy, soiled hands grabbed his cloak. "Please, I don't want to die."

Du Fay looked down at her as if she were inhuman. His eyes showed no pity, no compassion. Turning to one of his soulless disciples, he said, "Gag her."

Tying the red cloth tightly around her mouth, they lifted her naked body onto the altar and undid the chains. Her bruised arms and legs were held down by four hooded disciples as Du Fay began to utter his unholy words of evocation. Her eyes screamed out for help as she watched him take the dagger in both hands and raise it above her breasts.

"I call upon the dark angel, hatred of good, master of evil, show yourself."

The flames of the black candles dulled. The room became icy cold as the smell of death laid heavy in the hellish air. He lifted the dagger, stretching his merciless arms straight above his head. His savage hands grasped the neck of the razor sharp knife. He watched the terrified girl take her last breath of life as he threw his arms down, plunging the blade into her chest. He grabbed her wrist and sliced it, letting her blood drain into the silver chalice.

Holding the chalice of blood into the air, Du Fay charged the Evil Spirit again, his command echoing around the room. "Dark angel of destruction, this is your blood, draw from its life-force. You have been called. I am your master, and I command that you show yourself to me."

All at once, a red mist began to rise above the altar and within seconds the red-eyed beast appeared. Its reptile tail stood high behind its hideous demon face. Its black wings spread open as it moved forward. Du Fay stood back and uttered his command, and the beast began to disappear back into the floor.

His disciples watched in awe. Their master had once again proven he was Satan's chosen one. Du Fay's servants had given their souls to the devil in exchange for wealth and power. He had shown them the lust and excitement of sexual magic, taught them to enjoy the decadence of their sins. He departed the room leaving his servants to get rid of the dead girl. He was pleased. Tonight he had served his father well.

CHAPTER NINE

NICHOLAS AWAKENS

*H*ow can one describe that moment of loss, when the world disappears in a blink of an eye? How can one describe that moment of pain when you inhale such shock and devastation that you never find a way to exhale again? You can't. When I learned Elena had been murdered, everything I lived for became my every reason to want to die. For forty-eight hours, I was trapped in a state of collapse and shock, trying to think straight, trying to comply with the police and their demands. A haze of investigations, a haze of detectives marched in and out of our home until they were convinced that I was innocent.

It wasn't until I was allowed to bring Elena's embalmed body home that I knew it was safe to begin my chase to find her killer. Up the stairs I carried the love of my life and laid her down as if she were sleeping.

The merciless wounds on her breast were now hidden beneath the white lace dress I had taken to the coroner. I lifted the veil that covered her beaten and scarred face. A sea of guilt filled my chest as I begged her soul to forgive my vampire heart. I had asked her to be with me. I had promised her the stars. I had tried to protect her, but I had let go of her hand. My angel had fallen into the arms of a murderer, a deranged psychopath who had tortured her to death. For all my powers and all my strength, I wasn't there to save her when she'd needed me most.

"I'm so sorry," I cried. "So sorry, Elena. I should have protected you. I should have known. I should have. I should . . . Oh God." I broke down.

Tomorrow her body was to be taken back to London, where I knew her family would have wanted her to be laid to rest. Placing a rose upon her pillow, I imagined her soul in a field of flowers.

For the next few hours, I lay beside her, holding her as if she might open her eyes. She didn't. She didn't. My powers, my prayers could not make such a miracle happen. I kissed her bruised cheek, not wanting to leave her side. Closing my eyes, I stayed with her. For a while, I drifted in a void of emptiness.

Then the smell of flowers awoke my darkness. I wasn't dreaming when I witnessed her heaven. I wasn't dreaming when I felt her soul. Together I found us lying on a bed of roses, a mass of red roses that filled her room. A blanket of rose petals covered Elena's white dress, and the wounds on her beaten face had all disappeared.

"Elena," I said, softly, trying to wake her. But still she lay lifeless beneath the wings of eternity. I could feel her spirit drift through my body, hear her whisper her immortal love. It was a moment of light, a moment of hope, a moment of forever that would never fade away. Elena was my life. Elena was my love. Elena was my world, and that would never change.

The following evening I said goodbye through a blur of tears as I watched her white casket being placed in the hearse. Beneath the flickering street lamp, I stared at the horses' feather plumes portraying a scene so surreal and inconceivable that I held onto the railings for fear I might stumble. Like the sand in an hourglass, I saw my world empty as the horses lifted their hooves and carried my angel away into the distance. Weak and unsteady, I sat outside on the steps of our memories and waited for nothing except my sanity.

It wasn't until I dragged myself up that I noticed a crumpled piece of paper that had blown and got caught between one of the railings. I picked it up and went back inside the house. Throwing the paper into the waste basket, I left the drawing room. Then something urged me to turn around. An urgency, a warning grasped my stomach. My instincts were telling me to return to the room. I stood for a minute, wondering what it could be. There was no evidence of danger, but something was wrong. My eyes checked the corners of the room, the windows, the fireplace, the clock, the furniture. I waited for a sign, and then it happened. I saw Elena's quill left on the mantel by the clock. Looking down at the crumpled letter lying in the waste basket, I realized my instincts were telling me to read it. I opened the crinkled soiled paper and immediately recognized Elena's handwriting. My heart, my mind became lost in rage as I ran my fingers across the smudged stained message. I felt sick with anguish, knowing her letter had been thrown away and had been left undetected next to our house. Boucher, the necklace, Du Fay's evil plan! It all became clear. Elena had been tricked. A rage of frustration burnt through my veins as I blamed myself for not warning her about Du Fay. I should have told her my suspicions about him. I should have listened to my vampire instincts.

Locked inside the walls of my grief, I continued to question my ignorant mistakes. If I had known for one second the kind of monster Du Fay was, I would never have presumed time was on my side. Though the letter did not prove Du Fay had killed her, I knew in my veins that he was guilty. It was all too late. Too late to save the woman I loved. Too late to save our unborn child. Boucher was his accomplice. She had planned her every move, making sure to be away when the police went to speak to her. They had interviewed her butler who told them she'd left to visit a sick friend. By the time he'd finished answering their questions, the police were certain Boucher had nothing to do with Elena's murder. I'd asked them to tell me where she had gone, but they refused, insisting it was best I let them do their job. Trembling with anger, I pushed the letter in my pocket and raced across the square to find out where Boucher had disappeared. Banging on the door, I waited for her butler to appear. Then pushing him aside, I stormed into the house.

"Where is she?" I demanded. "Where is the Countess? Tell me now."

Standing against the wall, his deceitful eyes watched nervously. "Madame is not here. I don't know where she is."

Grabbing his neck, I said, "I know you are lying! Tell me where she is or I swear I will kill you."

He looked into my eyes, and I knew they were flaming. "Please," he gasped. "I am only following my orders."

Bearing my fangs, I gave him one last chance. "Don't make me have to kill you."

Crying with panic, he choked out, "She's in Cornwall. She left three days ago."

"And Du Fay? Is he there too?"

"I don't know." He trembled.

Looking into his corrupted face, I said, "If you are lying, you know what I'm going to do."

"I'm not lying. Please believe me."

I left him cowering on the floor and rushed across the square to where my carriage waited. I knew it was best to let my driver take me to Versailles. If by chance Du Fay was home, I needed to preserve what little strength I had. For the past few nights, the rats in the cellar were my source of blood. There had been too many police, too much commotion to allow me to leave the house freely. Clasping Elena's letter, I felt sick with fury as we began to head west out of the city. Soon we were rumbling our way through the black, deserted countryside. I checked my watch. "Faster," I snapped.

My driver drove the horses hard and fast. We were getting closer, but without clear directions, I knew finding Du Fay's house was not going to be easy. It wasn't until we hit the outskirts of Versailles that I suddenly noticed an opening in the trees ahead. "Slow down," I shouted, sensing a lead. Scanning the ground, I could now see carriage marks imprinted in the muddy earth, an unmarked path through the woods. We were here; I knew it. I could feel it in my gut. Ordering my driver to stop, I rushed out and told him to wait until I returned. Nervous and confused, he didn't dare defy me. He didn't ask where I was going. He just followed my orders.

Away from the carriage I flew through the trees. A storm of visions flashed through my mind as I thought about Elena being tortured and killed. I began to notice the woods were clearing. Then out in the distance, I saw Du Fay's domain. Like a fortress of evil, it possessed the night sky, a sleeping monster awaiting its next victim. The towering, black gates waited in silence as I leapt over them and proceeded toward the house. Seething with anger, I banged on the door.

"Du Fay," I shouted. "Come out and face me." Stepping back, I was ready to smash through one of the windows. Then all at once, the door opened, and his butler appeared.

His lying eyes glared, showing no fear. "The master is not here," he announced coldly.

Tearing past him into the hall, I felt the air thicken. I could taste its evil. "Du Fay," I bellowed, ready to destroy him. "I said come out and face me!"

The heavyset butler didn't panic or try to stop me. He just watched coolly, ignoring my rage. "I have already told you my master is not here. He is out of town. I don't expect him back for two weeks."

Too furious to listen, I began searching the house, smashing anything that reflected Du Fay's warped, perverse mind. Up the spiral staircase I ran. I chased down the corridors, checking every room of every floor of the house. No one was around, no servants, no maids. Racing back down the stairs, I looked for the butler, and then suddenly I was struck hard on the back of the head.

Twisting around, I saw him jump out, swinging a silver poker like a deranged madman. Lashing out again, he yelled back at me, "My master warned me you'd come here, but you are too late. The girl is dead."

Pulling the poker out of his hands, I grabbed his jaw, lifting him off the floor. "You saw Elena? You saw her come here with Boucher?" Hurling him across the hall, I watched his body smash into the large gold mirror, then drop to the floor. He tried to get up. His eyes filled with horror as I grabbed him again, allowing him to face his worst nightmare.

"Stop," he cried out. "I didn't know he was going to kill her. That wasn't the plan, but the girl would not listen."

"Listen to what?" I demanded.

"The girl refused to do what my master asked her. That is all I know. I am not lying. I will tell you where he is if you'll let me live!"

"Tell me!" I roared, shaking the answer out of him.

"He's in Cornwall," he cried. "They are all in Padstow. He has a house near there! His disciples are with him." He continued to squirm. "I only did what my master told me to do. If I didn't obey him, he'd kill me."

Feeling my body freeze with anger, I held him up against the wall. "Are you telling me the truth"?

"Yes, yes," he gasped, believing I might spare his life. His eyes expressed relief for one sickening second until I twisted his neck and felt it snap. Tearing my teeth into his flesh, I drank his blood, blinded by hate. For the first time, my pain had outweighed my conscience, and the blood of a sinner became my life-force. Only then did I realize the power of human blood. It was a force, a strength I could never have imagined.

Driving back to Paris, I didn't question what I had done. I was a vampire, not a murderer. I was a hunter, not a slayer. Du Fay was my target, not the helpless and innocent. Tomorrow at sunset, I'd journey to Cornwall. Unable to face going back to the house, I asked my driver to take me to St. Germain. Wandering alone, I thought about Elena, lost in a haze of memories and emptiness. The once familiar cafes and shops now felt unfamiliar without her. The sound of the church bells rang once then faded. I walked toward the pointed arches of a small church ahead. Staring up at the heavy, carved doors, my heart longed to walk inside. I wanted to pray. I wanted to kneel down at the altar, to light a candle for Elena and find a moment of peace. Tears of despair filled my eyes as I stared at the richly painted windows and became lost in the panes of art that portrayed great Saints. The power of faith breathed from its doors, but the light of its healing didn't heal me.

I heard a voice call out from a nearby building across the street. Turning around, I saw an old man wave out from his window. "Please wait," he called. I waited and watched him come out onto the street. Catching his breath, he smiled warmly. "Forgive me if I startled you, but when I saw you pass by, I wasn't sure if it was you."

For a moment, I didn't recognize him. Taking off his cap, he held it to his chest. "You don't remember me, do you?" he asked softly. "I am Francis, the violin player you gave the emeralds to." His words drifted through me as I thought about Elena.

"Yes, of course," I said, trying to conceal the pain I was feeling. "How are you Francis?"

"Because of you, my friend, I am well," he answered. "I have found a place to live, over there." He pointed back down the street. "It's a little shop with a room above. I have begun giving violin lessons there."

Nodding quietly, I tried to smile when all the while I wanted to sit down and weep.

The old man looked up sensing something was wrong. "Nicholas," he said, remembering my name. "What is wrong, my friend?"

I hesitated. "Nothing."

He appeared genuinely concerned. "I hope you don't mind me coming down here and talking to you, but I wanted to thank you again for what you did for me. That night when you stopped to help me, you changed my life. No one had cared when they saw me homeless, but you and your fiancée—two strangers I had never met before—appeared like angels on a cold winter's night. I shall never forget the miracle you gave me with such kindness, such magic. It's all beyond words."

His sincerity brought tears to my eyes. I was too choked to answer. "My friend, you are upset. If I have said something wrong, I didn't mean to."

"No, it's not you," I assured him.

"Then what is it?" he asked. "If you need someone to listen, I am here. You can trust me."

I didn't answer. There was no doubt Francis was a kind man, but still he was a stranger, a musician I had helped.

Stepping closer, Francis placed his hand on my arm. "Please," he asked, "At least let me offer you a warm drink. It is not good to be standing out here in the cold. I have a warm fire, some wine. If you are hungry, I have food."

His simple offering made me feel wanted, and God only knew how much I needed a friend. "All right," I answered him.

"Good," he said, and before I could change my mind, he led me inside the small, red door of his shop and up the stairs into his living room. "Please sit," he said, pulling up an extra chair at his table. Placing another log on the fire, he continued to try and make me feel welcome. "You are the first friend to join me up here in my home. I still cannot believe that I really live here," he added. Fetching a jug of red wine and two glasses, he placed them on the table. Then wiping his hands, he brought out a plate of cheese and bread. "Please eat, if you are hungry," he said, pouring us some wine.

Thanking him, I couldn't help but notice how clean and organized he kept his small home. From the bookcase in the corner to the little kitchen area where he prepared his meals, everything was neatly arranged. Even the inexpensive ornaments upon his mantel were polished and placed beneath the unschooled portrait of a kind-faced woman. Under his window was a large trunk with a red seat cushion placed on top. I noticed his violin left out on the seat and guessed he must have put it there when he'd rushed out to see me. Across the small wooden table, Francis broke a little bread and cheese onto a plate and offered it to me. Not wanting to offend him, I thanked him and continued to drink my wine. His kind eyes looked at me as he lifted his glass.

"To friendship," he said. "To your kindness, Nicholas."

For a while, it felt good to let someone else's energy break through my darkness. Francis was a good soul. His spirit reflected simple warmth, the kind of innocent honesty a child brings to a room. I watched him walk over to put away his violin. Carefully, he placed it back in its case as if he were laying a baby in its crib.

Turning to me, he smiled. "It is such a luxury to be able to play and teach downstairs in my shop. I also fix and sell used violins. Yesterday, I was able to give two violins to the local hospital. As much as I loved playing in the square, it was hard having to perform in the cold winter months. I am not as young as I used to be." He coughed. "Time is a thief, Nicholas," he said playfully, then coughed again. Taking a sip of his wine, he sighed reflectively. "Yesterday, I was young. Today, I am old. Believe me," he said softly, "that is how it feels sometimes." Standing his violin case safely in the corner, he walked to the hearth and warmed his hands.

"Do you teach every day?" I asked, trying not to appear distraught.

"No, not every day," he said humbly. "Right now, I only have four students, all of them children. Their parents insist they learn the violin, when all the while I see they'd much rather be playing in the park." He smiled. "It's funny, each one of them is so different, and yet they all have one thing in common. They all hate the violin." He chuckled. "I try to make it fun for them, but still it's beyond me why they are forced to play against their will. Music is a gift, a gift of expression. It shouldn't be a requirement. A child will tell you when their heart draws them to an instrument. "

He poured some more wine and sat back at the table. The more I listened to him, the more I warmed to his easy manner. I couldn't help but admire his willingness to continue working. Most elderly people who had spent their lives struggling to earn their living would have used the emeralds to retire in comfort. Francis, on the other hand, hadn't done that. His passion for music out-weighed any amount of money he'd been given. Even the little shop and home he had chosen were modest, simple and small. Noticing me staring at the plump-faced woman in the portrait above the mantel, his eyes filled with adoration.

"That is Sarah, my late wife," he said, softly. "How I miss that smile." He sighed. "There isn't a day that goes by that I don't miss her. Though many years have passed since I lost her, I can still hear her voice, still see her dancing and selling fruit in the square." He looked at her painting as if she were listening.

"To me, my Sarah was Paris and all its wonders. Tell me Nicholas, how is your fiancée? Are you planning to marry here in Paris?"

Overcome with emotion, I stared down into the rim of my glass. "Francis," I said, "my fiancée was found murdered three days ago here in Paris."

Gasping with shock, the elderly man replied, "Forgive me Nicholas, I'm so sorry. I'm so, so sorry." Leaning forward he gently folded his fingers around my hand. "Do the police know who did this?"

"No," I answered, "but tonight I came across something that proves where Elena went that day and who killed her."

"Have you told the police?"

"No, I haven't. They've already made mistakes. I'm not going to let them try to interfere and stop me from doing what needs to be done."

"Nicholas, I understand the pain you must be going through, but do you really think this is a wise decision?"

"I realize to you it doesn't make sense, and I appreciate your concern, but if you knew what I know

now, if you knew the way this psychopath works, you'd understand why I must hunt him alone."

Across the melting candle, Francis' eyes filled with worry. "Who is this man you speak of Nicholas? How do you know him?"

Pausing for a moment, I wondered if I should tell him.

"Nicholas," he said taking my hand. "You can trust me. If I can help you in any way, I will. I am your friend."

I looked back and knew I could trust him. "His name is Du Fay, Victor Du Fay."

Francis' expression changed, and he looked as if he'd seen a ghost. "Do you mean Count Victor Du Fay who lives near Versailles?"

"You know him?" I asked, taken aback.

"No, I do not know him. I have only heard rumors about him, terrible evil rumors, Nicholas. Some say he worships the devil and that he uses young girls to do the devil's work."

"How did you find this out?"

He sighed. "I have reached the winter of my life. These streets, these people, have become my world. The wind whispers many secrets when one spends his life working the sidewalks of Paris. If the stories I have heard are true, then this Du Fay character is not only dangerous, he is indestructible."

"No one is indestructible," I said. "What stories have you heard to make you think this?"

"I have heard he practices black magic and that his power and money get him whatever he desires. Young girls who walk the streets desperate for money have gone missing whenever his royal black coach crawls the night. Invisible eyes have seen the same silver crest upon the doors, the same red plumes that dress the finely groomed horses. Some say he uses jewelry and large amounts of money to lure his victims into his carriage."

"But what about the police? Surely they would have investigated the girls who went missing. Someone must have said something to the police. It doesn't make sense."

"Someone did tell the police about Du Fay. They investigated him two years ago."

"And what happened?"

"From what I heard, when the police visited his house, they found no evidence. No proof of anything. It was said the detective who was in charge of the case became quite friendly with Du Fay. Within a few months after the investigation, he came into a lot of money and decided to retire from the police force."

"But what about the missing girls? What about their families? The people that knew these women? Didn't anyone question what the police were doing about it?"

"Yes." Francis nodded, disheartened. "A brother of one of the missing girls was convinced Du Fay had taken his sister and was determined to make the police question him again. The police had told him they believed his sister may have just run away, but he refused to accept their opinion. Apparently it was he who told the police about Du Fay in the first place."

"So did he convince the police to interview Du Fay again?"

"No, he didn't," Francis sighed, shaking his head. His eyes stared into the bottom of his glass. "It was horrible, Nicholas. This poor young man, who had done nothing but try and help the police, was found dead on the steps of the cathedral in the square. His head had been severed and his tongue cut out. I pray I will never have to witness anything like that again. I remember standing amongst the whispering crowd as the rain began to fall on the bloodstained steps of the church. It was as if the devil were watching over us. A silent evil that seemed to hang in the air. Though no evidence pointed to Du Fay being involved, it left an unspoken fear in the hearts of those who'd heard about him. It seemed after that anyone who suspected him became too scared to even mention his name."

I pictured Elena and how Du Fay had tortured her. Trembling inside, I couldn't wait to kill him.

Nicholas," Francis whispered, "I'm sorry I had to tell you all this, but I feel it is my duty as your friend to explain what I know."

"You don't have to apologize. I understand your reasons. Believe me, nothing you've said could make things any worse. What you have told me only confirms that the only way to kill this monster is to hunt him alone. Tonight, I found out Du Fay is in Cornwall. He has a house near Padstow. I'm leaving tomorrow to go there."

Francis looked at me, his eyes filled with admiration. "You have a warrior's heart, Nicholas, and a God-given gift. In all my years, I have never met anyone like you."

Feeling unworthy of such a compliment, I only wished that God was on my side. As the flames of the fire began to die out, I realized the time was nearing 4:00 a.m. Standing up, I thanked him for his hospitality.

"Don't feel you have to leave " he said, pulling himself up from the table. "You can rest here if you wish. I have some spare blankets."

"Thank you, but I must leave now."

Rubbing his tired eyes, Francis insisted on seeing me downstairs to the door. "Promise me, you'll come and see me when you return, Nicholas. Travel safe, my friend, and may God bless the courage that guides your soul."

Carrying the warmth of Francis' words, I promised him I'd see him on my return.

CHAPTER TEN

MY JOURNEY TO CORNWALL

"If you bring forth what is within you, it will save you.
If you do not bring forth what is within you, what you
do not bring forth will destroy you."

Gospel of Thomas.

Was a black magician more powerful than a vampire?
I did not know. Was power without heart Du Fay's
strength or weakness? I was not sure. These questions
stayed with me as my boat drifted away from the tireless
harbor. Accepting my fate and trials had made me see the
truth without excuses. Being different didn't change the
rules of good and evil. We are who we choose to be. I was
a vampire who still believed in justice. I was a man who
still believed in love. God had forsaken me, but my faith
still remained. Whatever my future, whatever my sins, I
knew in my heart that the devil did not control me.

My journey to Cornwall proved long and hard. Traveling alone, avoiding the sunlight, finding inns that met the needs of a vampire proved much more difficult than I'd imagined. Paying generously had helped, but still it was difficult surviving on rats, awakening disoriented, realizing I was lying in some strange run-down room. From sea to land, it had not been easy, but when we finally reached Devon, I began to feel a sense of relief. Though a storm had thrown our carriage off the jolting road, and the driver insisted we wait until morning, I did not panic. Padstow wasn't far, but I needed to find shelter. I had less than an hour before sunrise. The driver had mentioned an inn a few miles ahead, the Malster's Arms. Fighting against the Cornish gales, I struggled across the dangerous countryside. Over the stubborn hills toward the sea, I continued to follow the directions I'd been given. Out in the distance, I spotted a tavern about half a mile from the treacherous ocean.

The thick, salty air stung my eyes as I battled to see through the hail and rain. Catching my breath, I forced myself forward, thinking about the countless seamen who had perished on this untamable coast. Beneath the flashing black sky, the wind howled and cried like a thousand wolves over the haunting cliffs. Shivering wet, I finally reached the inn, banging on the door, desperate for cover. Yelling out for the innkeeper, I heard the door unbolt. Then all at once it opened, and a large, bearded man helped pull me inside. His hard, weathered face was unmoved as he offered me a chair and poured me a brandy. Staring down unsympathetically, he threw a shot of brandy down his throat. "Coach break down, did it?" he grunted.

"Yes," I answered him, shivering from the cold.

Passing me a blanket, he shook his head. "I don't know why you city people underestimate this deadly coast. The churchyards are full of sailors pulled dead from these riotous waters, caught by an onshore wind and a rising tide with two thousand miles of Atlantic behind it."

He poured me another brandy and pushed his guestbook across the table. "You'll have to sign in. I've a room ready. You can pay me later." Sinking with exhaustion, I signed my name. "There's some left over stew if you're hungry."

"No, thank you," I answered. "Just a room and some extra blankets will do."

"All right then," he said firmly. Up the crooked stairs, he led me into a damp-smelling room. "No one will bother you," he said. "And I shouldn't worry. The storm should pass in a few hours. Where are you heading?"

"Padstow," I replied.

"No problem. If the weather proves fair, I'll take you there myself. I am going there tomorrow," he said. As he closed the door behind him, I waited for him to go downstairs then locked the door. Drawing the worn curtains, I hung my cloak over the small window, and lay down, too tired to think.

By the time I awoke, daylight had disappeared. The storm had settled, and the innkeeper did as he said and took me to Padstow. The night was still young, and as we arrived into the busy port, I could already smell the blood of drunken sailors that filled the brisk air. I was hungry

and determined to track down Du Fay, but first I needed
to regain my strength.

Though I'd decided never to drink the blood of the
innocent, the blood of the wicked was now open prey.
Thanking the innkeeper, I paid him well, and strolled ahead
down the noisy street. Following my senses, I absorbed the
night, watching and listening to find my next victim.

Padstow was alive with hard-faced seamen with
foreign accents that carried across the torch-lit water. I
chose to stop at one of the less chaotic inns and arrange
a room for later that night. From there I crossed the
street to another tavern, noticing the place seemed full of
locals. Sitting down at a quiet table, I thought about Du
Fay and wondered why he needed to be in Cornwall. A
short, round barmaid brushed by my chair, clearing one
of the tables next to me.

Turning to a couple by the window, she said, "Isn't
it terrible about the Morgan child going missing? Little
Johnny. Who would have thought it?"

The husband nodded taking a sip of ale. "Aye, I
heard about it today. Still no news then?"

"No," the barmaid answered, resting her tray down
on the table. "I do hope they find him." She shook her
head sadly. "He was such a nice boy, the face of an angel."

The man's wife at the table spoke up sharply. "Well
it doesn't surprise me, having a mother like that. It's a
wonder the child could survive at all."

"Hush, Rose," her husband insisted.

Ignoring him, she continued to get angry, "Six boys
to six different fathers. If she stopped her drinking . . ."

"Rose, that's enough," her husband interrupted again. "This isn't about the boy's mother. Let's just hope the police find him alive."

The barmaid nodded, picking up her tray. "You're right, Ted. Bessy may have her faults, but she still loves those boys. Let's just pray the police find him."

As the barmaid walked away, an old woman who'd been listening spoke out across the room. "It's the devil at work," she shouted. "I've seen him," she said, clasping her withered hands around her ale. The locals didn't respond, ignoring her comment, but I sensed the old woman was telling the truth. "He's out there," she cried out again. "Up on that hill, and every time he comes here, a child goes missing."

"Who, Mary?" the barmaid asked.

"The devil, that's who!" She pointed out the window.

The innkeeper expressed his amusement. "Come now, Mary. I think you've had enough ale tonight. You'll be warning us of werewolves next."

"You can all laugh, but mark my words, my gypsy blood can still see the evil in a man's eyes."

"And who might this man be, Mary?" another regular asked with humor in his voice.

"He's the one who came in here three nights ago buying everyone drinks. That rich stranger with the eyes of the devil."

"Oh Mary." The innkeeper laughed. "You don't mean the Frenchman, Victor Du Fay, do you? Why you couldn't get a more polite, generous gentleman than Victor. As I recall, you didn't refuse your free brandy." He grinned and shook his head.

Sipping her ale, she sat back in her chair and pulled her shawl defensively around her shoulders. "Mock all you want," she mumbled, "but I know I'm right."

Glancing around the room, I watched everyone go back to their conversations and newspapers. It was as if the old woman had suddenly become invisible. No one had believed a word she'd said, least of all the innkeeper, who'd actually defended Du Fay.

Leaving my table, I went to the bar. The innkeeper looked up as if asking what I wanted.

"I am an old friend of Victor Du Fay," I said, and he looked surprised.

"I apologize for the old woman's outburst," he said. "She gets carried away with all her gypsy suspicions."

"It didn't bother me," I replied. "Do you know where my friend is staying?"

"I'm not sure," he answered. "In fact, I think he told me he was planning to leave yesterday, or it could have been the day before. I can't remember now."

Looking into his shifty eyes, I knew he was lying, so I began reading his mind. Du Fay was in Wadebridge, staying in a house up on the cliffs somewhere near the Black Horse Inn.

He poured me another brandy, insisting it was on him. "So what brings you to Padstow?" he asked.

"Nothing in particular. Just passing through," I answered casually. "Sad about the missing boy. Do you know his mother?"

"Yes." He nodded, lowering his voice. "But between you and me, what happened doesn't surprise me. Bessy's a drinker. She doesn't know where she is half the time. Those young boys of hers stay out 'til dark, messing around on the docks. It's not good." He shook his head. "When you live in a busy port like this, you soon realize how dangerous it can be. A different ship every other night; you can't trust these foreigners. They'd rob you as look at you. No, you can't trust them. Not with our women, let alone our children."

Feeling my blood boil, I could see behind his mercenary eyes. He'd been assisting Du Fay each time he came to Padstow. The innkeeper had become Du Fay's informer, guiding him to children from desperate, pitiful backgrounds. Three children in three years, all of them still missing, all of them boys. The locals trusted this man. He was a part of their community, a part of their lives. Listening to his lies, I controlled my outrage, leading him into a sense of false security. I'd already decided he was going to die, maybe not tonight, but before I left Cornwall. Just then, two fishermen burst into the pub, rowdy and drunk, looking for trouble. Shouting to be served, they stared around at the inoffensive regulars who tried to ignore them.

"I haven't seen you in a while," the barmaid commented, handing them a couple of ales.

"Does that mean you've missed me?" one of them asked, grabbing her arm.

Not bothering to reply, she smiled sarcastically and went about her work. His shark-like eyes drifted across the bar, then all at once, I noticed him looking at my ring. As he turned back to his friend, I could see their cunning faces planning to follow me once I left. It could not have been easier, an empty dark alleyway with two cut-throat thieves. Their blood would be my strength, my weapon to kill Du Fay.

Finishing my drink, I saw one of them snigger and point to a table across the room. "Isn't that Paddy Farley and his crippled lad over there?" he whispered. "We haven't seen him since the night his missus died in that fire. He still owes me some money."

Watching the young boy and his father get up to leave, I listened as the same fisherman made a sick joke about the boy's twisted foot. A terrible sadness hung over the father, and his shadowed eyes dipped hopelessly beneath his tattered, gray cap. Holding his son's arm, he gave him his cane and fixed his scarf to walk outside. Pretending to be friendly, the same cruel drunk walked over and stopped them. "Hello Paddy," he said standing in front of the doorway.

Placing his hand around his son's shoulder protectively, the boy's father tipped his cap and tried to pass.

"Not so fast," the fisherman said, still keeping his voice low. "I haven't seen you since the night of that fire when you left the Anchor without paying me my money."

The boy's father looked surprised. "What money?" he asked.

"The money you owe me, that's what."

I could see that the boy's father was telling the truth. "Please, I don't want any trouble," he answered, shaking with fear. "You must have me mixed up with someone else."

"Listen here, Farley," the fisherman said. "It doesn't bother me that you left your missis to die in that fire, and it doesn't bother me that Billy here ended up a cripple because you were too drunk to help him, but what does bother me is when you think you can steal from me. I know where you live, Paddy. You don't want to end up a cripple like Billy? Do you? Or maybe Billy might have another bad fall. You wouldn't want that would you?"

"Why are you doing this? I don't owe you any money," the father answered desperately.

"Well, I say you do, and I'll be waiting in here tomorrow night to get it."

Clenching my fists, I wanted to break him, make him apologize and throw him out on the street. The bullying fisherman was going to die; he was going to find out what fear truly felt like. I finished my drink and walked outside. The two fishermen followed, planning their attack. It didn't take long for me to find a quiet street, sensing the two thieves ready to pounce. As they whispered to each other, I heard one of them mention a blocked tunnel ahead. Playing them at their own game, I turned around, acting the part of a frightened gentleman. Lifting my feet, I began to run.

"Get him," they yelled, and began chasing after me like two mad dogs. Spotting the passageway, I turned inside, leapt up on top of the roof, and watched them enter.

"You keep watch," the main culprit said. "He can't escape. It's a dead end in here." He pulled his jagged knife from the side of his boot, and his hefty arms swung out in the dark, prepared to slash anything that moved.

"Hurry up," the other one gasped, checking the street to check if anyone was coming.

Like a silent shadow, I dropped to the ground and grabbed his accomplice, breaking his neck. Leaving his body inside the passageway, I heard the other fisherman call out from the end of the tunnel. "Ray, is that you? Have you got him?"

Leaping back up to the roof, I crawled down the tunnel like a spider in the dark. Again the fisherman called out to his friend as he waved his knife, searching the passageway. Checking him from above, I allowed the red mist of my protection to follow him down the tunnel like a sea of blood.

"What's happening? Ray, where are you?" he called out, panicking. Above the mist, I growled, allowing him to see the nightmare before him. Hanging upside down, I clenched my teeth revealing the canine daggers that were about to tear him apart. The fisherman screamed and fell back into the mist. He shouted in terror, slicing the air with his knife.

"Get away from me! Whatever you are, don't come any closer!" Hungry for his blood, I descended to the ground. Bearing my fangs, I reveled in his fear. He shouted for his partner, still grasping his knife, cowering and crying like the coward he was.

"He's already dead," I informed him. "There's no one here to save you and no way out, remember?" Snatching his knife, I threw it aside and dragged him up, making him face me. "Look at me," I demanded. "Look into my vampire eyes, fisherman. How does it feel to be afraid? You should have left the crippled boy and his father alone."

Shaking with fright, he tried to answer, stuttering his words, crying with horror. "I . . . I will. . . leave them," he gasped, "just don't kill me."

"I'm not going to kill you yet." I smiled, squeezing my fingers into his red veined cheeks. "First I'm going to drink your blood. Then you will die."

"No," the fisherman yelled as I slammed him up against the wall and ripped my teeth into his neck. His screams faded fast as I drank his blood, feeling my body redeem its strength. Still conscious, he begged me silently with his eyes for mercy.

"Now you will die," I said, snapping his neck. I continued to feed until I felt my body filled with energy.

I'd consumed enough human blood to continue my hunt to kill Du Fay and whoever dared try to protect him. Leaving both fishermen dead in the tunnel, I stormed the Coastline ready for battle. No carriage could have taken me to Wadebridge faster than the speed of which I could now travel. Flying across the midnight sky, I scanned the land below. My instincts led the way like a map, guiding my body in the right direction. I was a vampire charged by human blood. Twice I'd experienced the extent of its power, but this time it was stronger, more intense than before. Gliding in the air like a large bird of prey, I searched the cliffs that led to Wadebridge. Above the crashing waves, through the freezing wind, I was persistent, tireless, steady and strong. Tonight Du Fay was going to burn in hell, and I was willing to burn with him to see justice done.

Again my body steered me toward my purpose, leading me down until I saw Du Fay's house standing on the cliffs. Its white pointed roof pierced the black sky through the haunting gray mist above the frothing sea. Once again, Du Fay had chosen a place that proved difficult to get to, especially in harsh weather. No carriage could have driven up a hill so steep unless the conditions proved dry and fair. Bolting downward above the house, I circled the walls, already feeling the devil inside. The deafening sound of the crashing waves made it easy to break in, and enter without being heard. Once inside, I began to search the lower level of the house.

They were all there, Du Fay and his followers. I could taste them, smell them, feel their sick presence. Proceeding up the stairs, I suddenly heard the faint sound of voices coming from one of the top floors. Their strange beckoning chants seemed to sway the house causing the lights to flicker and dim unnaturally. The deranged pictures on the walls now flashed eerily in the quivering low light. Women and beasts performing sexual acts, a hideous reflection of Du Fay's twisted mind.

Telling myself to remain focused, I tried to control my turmoil and rage. I hadn't come to Cornwall to make a mistake. Killing Du Fay wasn't going to be easy. I still had to get past his devil-worshipping servants who could give a coward like him time to escape. Quickly, I reached the top level of the house and drifted down the hall towards an arched, black door.

There were no other rooms on that floor, no windows, no lights, only a long dark corridor that felt like hell. A smell of death now hung in the air like the devil's breath upon my shoulder. Moving as a silent thief, I opened the door and peered around the room without being seen. Slipping inside the torch-lit temple, I stood back in the shadows waiting for Du Fay to appear. Thirteen of his followers waited before the altar, chanting and mumbling words in some mysterious language. Dressed in black hooded robes that hid their faces, they bowed their heads and awaited their leader. I was witnessing an underworld of organized evil, planned by a madman driven by self-worship.

His stage was set, lit with tall black candles. From the large Pentagram that hung behind the altar to the silver-jeweled chalice and dagger placed strategically at the end of the table, everything was laid out ready for the master. I saw what appeared to be a long pillow in the middle of the altar that was covered by a black and gold drape bearing the symbol of another pentagram.

The chanting stopped, and for the first time since Elena's death, I saw the murderer who had killed my angel. Through a hidden door in the wall, Du Fay appeared like a nightmare beyond nightmares that was now my reality. Trembling with rage, I relived every painful second of holding Elena's tortured dead body in my arms. Forcing myself not to lose my mind, I held back for the right moment to sneak up and kill him. My instincts were telling me to wait and observe.

Standing back in an unlit corner, I watched him approach the altar and raise his arms. He stared down at his overawed worshippers, his black marble eyes commanding the room. His gold and purple robe dramatized the ceremony, but Du Fay wasn't acting. There was nothing unreal about the effusion of evil flowing through the air. He lit some incense and began swinging it rhythmically above the altar, all the time whispering strange mystical words under his breath. His face became almost entranced as the smoke from the censor began to rise unnaturally.

Streaks of mist swirled into the air like dancing cobras rising out of a basket. The flames on the candles stretched freakishly high up toward the cloud of smoke that ladened the air with damnable energy. The smoke was now forming into a ball of mist, but there was something inside the reddish sphere that was beginning to take shape. Like black shining mirrors, Du Fay's eyes flashed with evil, his face fixed with concentration. I could see he had transcended himself to a higher level of consciousness, his dazed expression lost in the moment. My instincts were still warning me not to move forward, but this time I didn't listen as I began to slip quietly toward the altar. I didn't use my vampire speed. Instead I moved cautiously never once taking my eyes off Du Fay. His disciples remained mesmerized, none of them noticing me pass in the shadows. It wasn't until one of them got up to assist him that another of his servants saw me.

"Master, an intruder," she screamed. "A spy!"

All at once, Du Fay saw me racing toward him. "Kill him," he ordered, grasping the dagger. He leapt off the altar, his eyes burning with rage as I fought his disciples who attacked like a pack of wild dogs.

One by one, I threw them through the air as they punched and scratched, biting, and kicking. Suddenly Du

Fay struck me from behind, stabbing me in the shoulder as he yelled out, "Someone protect the altar."

Twisting around, I went to grab him, feeling his powers forcing me back.

"You can't win," he roared. "Your vampire powers aren't strong enough to challenge the master." At that moment, I felt our energies collide like forks of lightning that lit the room.

His servants backed away, and his eyes blazed with anger as he lashed out again. This time I caught the knife, slicing his arm in the struggle, still trying to break through the force of his volition. Will against will, strength against strength, we battled across the floor like two wild beasts. His demonic soul now showed on his face, distorting his features like the devil's own son.

A clash of two horrors shook the walls, a vampire against a black magician, both of us unstoppable. Hungry to kill him and rip out his throat, I felt my fangs flash like daggers ready to strike. Du Fay didn't give up. His powers didn't weaken, but as he grasped his arm, panic rushed through his black eyes. His cut was deep, blood now gushing through his fingers. He wanted to escape, but he knew he couldn't.

Ready to finish him, my vampire eyes slammed the door closed to keep him prisoner. Justice was mine. I was stronger than strong. My wounds had healed. My powers hadn't failed me. Du Fay's shield of will was about to fall, leaving him unprotected to burn in hell. It wasn't until I heard a child's cries behind me that suddenly my purpose became a whirlwind of human emotion. Spotting the naked boy screaming on the altar, I couldn't believe

what Du Fay had done. A satanic beast had risen out of
the smoke, its hairy body now descending to the floor.
Towering over the boy, its evil breath panted through
its wet gapping nostrils, ready to take the child. With
forehooves raised, its repulsive head bore a sharp beard
and two arched horns resembling those of a goat. It was
that second, that moment, that Du Fay and his followers
became insignificant. An innocent child was about to be
taken, and saving his life was all I cared about.

Charging through the air, still grasping the dagger, I
heard Du Fay's voice explode across the room. Everything
I was and everything I'd become, joined together into a
weapon of faith. I was a vampire that still believed in
God, and God only knew how much I needed him now.
Summoning all my strength, I slammed the dagger into
the beast, twisting the blade through its chest.

"No," Du Fay roared. "What have you done? You've
destroyed this night. You've destroyed my work."

Seeing the beast squeal and twist, I felt its powers trying
to steal my strength, but as it began to disintegrate, so did its
power. Du Fay and his disciples screamed out in shock.

"Kill him, stop him," Du Fay commanded. "Don't
let him take the boy. We can't let him get away."

All at once, they ran toward me salivating with rage,
obsessed with evil. Throwing the altar cloth around the
boy, I scooped him in my arms and flew up to the ceiling.

"Close your eyes," I whispered. "Nothing will harm
you now." His thin arms wrapped around my neck as he
buried his face into my shoulder. Above the screams and

mayhem, I charged toward the door, forcing it open with my fearless red eyes.

Out in the corridor, I thought we'd escaped, but again I was wrong as another two mad servants jumped out from the top of the stairs. Feeling one of them stab my arm, I shielded the boy like a determined father. It was difficult to fight while protecting him, but still I managed to kick the armed man down the stairs. Just then, Countess Boucher leapt in front of me, possessed with madness. Her twisted cruel mouth screamed out for the boy. Clawing my face, she fought like a man trying to tear the child out from my arms. With one hand, I grabbed her by the throat and squeezed the life out of her demonic face. Using her dead body like a human shield, I hurled it down the corridor to hold back the others.

Hugging the trembling child, I wanted to comfort him, but there was no time, no time! I needed to find him some blankets before heading out into the freezing night air. Flying down the stairs into one of the bedrooms, I saw the window to our escape. I locked the door, and laid him down, trying to calm him as I wrapped up his frail body. I knew this was the boy who'd gone missing in Padstow. I remembered his name, Johnny . . . Johnny Morgan.

"Johnny," I whispered. "I'm not here to harm you. I'm going to take you home. We'll escape through the window."

Frozen with terror, his innocent eyes stared in horror, too scared to answer, too scared to speak. That's when it hit me. What the hell was I thinking? I was a vampire. In all the panic, I'd forgotten how frightening

I must have appeared to him. Turning away, I felt like a monster. "Johnny," I said, "I know how terrified you must be but believe me, I would never hurt you. I'm not like the others."

At that moment, I heard someone running toward the door. "Come, we have to leave." I carried him to the window. "Trust me, Johnny, and close your eyes. I promise you I won't let you go." Overcome with emotion, I locked him in my arms, and together we flew into the bitter black sky.

Above the unforgiving sea, my heart wept for Elena as I held the boy as I would my own son. Tears stung my sunken cheeks. I could have been a father. I could have married the woman I loved. Our world had just begun, and then suddenly it was gone. Through the mist, I saw the sleepless harbor, and in a lost and desperate moment, I kissed the boy's forehead. As much as I yearned for him to return to his family, I didn't want to let him go. I didn't want to be alone. Asking my powers to give him strength, I took him to the hospital where I knew I had to leave him. I couldn't be seen taking him inside. I had done everything a vampire was capable of. Entering through the back of the building, I quietly laid him down safely where I knew he'd be found.

"Goodbye, Johnny," I whispered. "It's time for me to leave." His hand grasped my cloak, and his eyes reached up to me, not wanting me to leave. "It's all right" I whispered. Right then I heard a nurse approaching, and within that moment, I was gone. From the rooftop, I watched her rush to his side. The child was safe, but the sun was now rising.

Like a fugitive of light, I flew back to the inn and hurried to my room, shielding the windows, unable to rest as I thought about Du Fay. Saving the boy had left me vulnerable. I was shaken, disturbed by everything I'd witnessed. I thought about the altar and how I'd mistaken the child for a pillow beneath the cloth. He must have been drugged to remain so still. How, with all my powers, could I have been so blind? Over and over, I replayed it back in my mind. Du Fay, the devil. Countess Boucher. I recalled seeing two of the Countess's associates, remembering their faces from the ball in Versailles. Lord Trembly and the Professor, both possessed by the devil, following Du Fay's orders like obedient mad dogs. Desperate to return, I sat shaking with anger. Twelve more hours, and I was free to go back. Would Du Fay still be there? I did not know, but one thing was certain, our battle wasn't over. Losing the child had left him livid. It had crushed his authority in front of his followers. The destruction of the beast he had summoned from hell shattered the mirror of his indestructibility.

Already, I could feel his revengeful breath whispering threats inside my head. From dawn until sunset, I didn't sleep. Then out in the darkness, I returned to Wadebridge. Driven by fury, I flew into the house prepared to kill anything that stood in my way. As the voice of the ocean roared outside, an ungodly silence breathed within its walls. The unlit hallway now smelled of disinfectant. The furniture, the floor, everything had been cleaned and polished. Rushing upstairs, I checked the black corridor that led to the room where the beast had been summoned. Not one trace of evidence had been left behind. Du Fay and his disciples had covered their tracks perfectly. The heavy stone altar was gone. The satanic signs upon the walls had all been removed. Not one drop of blood stained the polished floor. Only the faint smell of incense still lingered in the air. Remembering the hidden door in the wall, I forced it open, discovering Du Fay's large, mirrored room. There too, he had left no evidence behind, except the aura of his cruel sadistic mind. Shaking with frustration, I felt defeated. He'd been able to get away, and there was nothing I could have done to stop him.

Back downstairs, I was ready to leave when I heard a noise coming from one of the downstairs rooms. Racing down the hall, I saw a light beneath the door. I burst forward and kicked it open. Straight away, I recognized the wicked innkeeper, the heartless coward who'd been helping Du Fay. Standing by the hearth, his eyes froze with panic as I discovered him burning the rest of the evidence. Spotting a child's shoe aflame on the fire, I stormed toward him as he tried to run. Hurling him across the room, I watched him crumble onto the floor. His blood was mine. He was going to hell. Brandishing my fangs unmercifully into his face, I remembered the boy on the altar. "This is what it feels like to be the victim," I growled.

"It wasn't me who took the boy," he screamed. "It was Du Fay! He needed another child. I just told him where to go. I needed the money. Please don't kill me."

"And what about Johnny Morgan?" I roared. "And all the others you helped kill. Did you think about their suffering? A defenseless child! Did you?" I shook him.

"Johnny Morgan's alive," he sobbed. "I heard he's in the hospital. Someone took him there last night."

"I know he's alive," I answered. "It was I who saved him."

"Please, I'm sorry," he cried. "I'll do anything, anything!"

"You'll do nothing." I yanked his head back, ignoring his screams as I ripped my teeth into his neck. Like Vampire wine, I drank his blood, full bodied and powerful. I felt it inflame my energy. Just as the moon controls the sea, the claret of life controlled my body.

Leaving his drained body on the floor, I set fire to the house and fled back to Padstow. I returned to the dead innkeeper's tavern where I knew the atmosphere wouldn't be chaotic. From hell and fury, I needed to think, regain my sanity after a whirlwind of madness. Lost in my emotions, I swallowed my frustration. So much had happened in the last twenty-four hours, but still I hadn't been able to kill Du Fay. Tomorrow at dusk, I'd begin my journey back to Paris, a journey I hoped wouldn't take too long. I asked the barmaid to bring me some port and sat in the corner alone with my thoughts.

As the light from the fireplace flickered across the old beams of the tavern, I wondered how I was ever going to accept my life without Elena. Sundown had become a nightmare that reminded me she was gone, and sunrise my relief as I slept through the pain of her absence. My only reason to want to live was to kill Du Fay, and then, nothing, only emptiness. I thought about my father and how Charlotte used to tell me that when he lost my mother, he lost himself. Only now did I understand his feelings of grief, but that was no excuse for the way he had treated me.

When Elena had told me we were having a child, my initial reaction was doubt and fear. Looking back, I realized she knew me better than I knew myself. Being a father could have given me a chance to heal my pain and love a child the way I'd wished I'd been loved.

Finishing my drink, I was getting ready to leave until I heard the barmaid mention Johnny Morgan.

"It's a miracle the boy's alive," she said to an older man across the bar. "They found Johnny left alone in the hospital, shivering cold with just a blanket around him. Supposedly, the poor boy was naked. No one knows who took him there or where he had been."

The gray-haired man shook his head. "It makes you wonder what the world is coming to. How could someone just leave a child alone suffering like that. It's sickening. Whoever it was must have known something."

"I know," the barmaid sighed. "When I saw his mother Bessy leaving the hospital today, she was crying with relief, but at the same time, she was worried sick. The doctor had told her Johnny's suffering from so much shock it may take months, even years, before he gets back to normal. When they'd asked him what he remembered, nothing he told them made any sense. He was talking about monsters and how some great beast had wanted to kill him."

"Poor lad," the old man replied. "It's a terrible thing, shock. He must have been scared out of his wits to be imagining things like that. Sounds to me like someone had given him a bad beating. Did he suffer any serious wounds?"

"No, I don't think so," she answered. "Just a few cuts and bruises. It's his memory they're worried about. Bessy said he just keeps imagining things he believes to be real. He even told her he'd flown across the sky to get to the hospital and that a good monster with red eyes and fangs had saved him. I must admit I do feel sorry for Bessy. I know she's not the best of mothers, but she does love her boys. Let's just pray Johnny gets better, eh."

"Aye." The old man nodded.

The barmaid poured herself a small gin and threw it down her throat as if taking a shot of medicine. "It's all so weird," she said nervously. "It seems this week's been one tragedy after another. First Johnny goes missing and comes back talking about monsters. And then Ayle Tremyne and Ray, two of our local fisherman, both found dead this morning, one with his neck broken and the other with his throat torn out. They were only in here last night. I just can't believe they're both dead."

The old man lit his pipe and sipped his ale. "Well, if you ask me, they both had it coming to 'em. Always wanting trouble, always picking fights, both of em gamblers and thieves." He paused, taking another puff on his pipe. "It's like the old saying goes, 'If you live by the sword, you die by the sword,' and I for one won't miss seeing 'em around."

"Come now, Lance. You shouldn't speak ill of the dead."

"There's nothing ill about the truth," he said firmly.

Listening to their conversation made me feel more at ease. At least the poor boy had remembered I'd tried to help him. Unfortunately though, no one would ever believe his story. Maybe in some ways it was best. The less the police questioned him, the easier it would be for him to try and move on. What Johnny needed now was to go home and be with his family.

As I got up to leave, I caught sight of Paddy Farley and the crippled boy pass by the window. I decided to help them and followed them down the street. Was I searching for some kind of forgiveness? I asked myself. Was I trying to convince myself I was still a good man? I didn't feel guilty about killing those men. I didn't feel bad about anything I had done. At the same time I knew, I had committed a string of murders, but I believed I had done the right thing.

Outside I watched the boy hobble down an uneven path and grasp his father's arm as they stopped to look at the boats on the harbor. From a distance, I observed the way Paddy Farley protected his son. There was no doubt how much he loved his little boy, but the weight of his guilt hung heavy on both of them. I could read his sorrow like an open book. Time had stood still since the night of the fire. Every day, he awoke to the same thoughts and regrets. If only he'd gone straight home instead of drinking that night. That one mistake had caused him to lose the woman he loved and left his boy a cripple. A double tragedy he had to accept.

While his son pointed to one of the ships sailing out the harbor, his father remembered when Billy would run down the docks to greet him. It was sad, so troubling to be able to read his despair. Paddy Farley had once stood tall and proud on the docks of Padstow, a hardworking fisherman, loyal to his family, honest with his friends. Now all that remained was a broken man unaware of how much his son missed his father who used to laugh and share stories of his days on the sea.

I wasn't sure if my powers could heal the boy, but I was going to try. As they began to walk away, I proceeded to follow them. It wasn't going to be easy for I knew Paddy Farley wouldn't trust a stranger with his boy. If I had to use force to hold him back, I was prepared to do so to try and heal the child. I had an idea, one I hoped might prove effective. Away from the busy harbor, they continued down a quiet side street and with no one else around, I approached them.

"Excuse me," I said. "I don't mean to bother you, but I'm a doctor. Justine's the name." I went to shake the father's hand, but Paddy Farley didn't return the gesture. He just nodded, waiting for me to finish. "I noticed you and your son in the tavern last night and wondered if you'd allow me to take a look at his foot. I think I might be able to help him.

Paddy Farley looked suspicious. "Thank you, but I'd prefer you didn't. My Billy's already seen three doctors. There's nothing anyone can do."

"I understand," I answered, "but I'm not a regular doctor. I am what you might call a spiritual healer. Maybe if Billy would allow me to hold him, I could use my faith to help him walk again. The boy's eyes widened, desperate with hope.

"Please Dad, let him try," he said. "He can heal me. Please let him try."

"Listen Billy," his father began, getting upset. "You know what the doctors said. There's nothing anyone can do." Turning to me, he tried to stay calm. "How can you say such things to a child? My son was crippled in a fire. He lost his mother. Isn't that enough, without you giving him false hope?"

"But Dad," his son cried out, "he said he could make me better. He said he could. Please let him try."

"No Billy, there's no such thing as a spiritual healer. Believe me, no one has prayed for a miracle more than I have. I love you, Billy. You know I wouldn't lie to you."

"Why don't you listen to your son?" I asked him. "He believes I can help him, and so do I."

"Billy." I leaned down to him. "Do you believe in miracles?

"Yes I do," he answered.

"Stop this," Paddy shouted. "Please just leave us alone."

Ignoring his father, I looked into the boy's eyes. I knew I could heal him, but while his father held him, a shield of negativity was making it impossible. "I know how much you love your boy," I told him, "but right now, I need you to stand back and let go of Billy's hand."

"I won't. You're not going near my son."

Not wanting to hurt him, I asked him again, this time using my powers to restrain him.

"You can't do this," he shouted, falling on the ground. "Don't hurt my boy," he cried out, unable to move.

Placing my hand around the child's ankle, I could see and feel how badly it was twisted. "You're a brave boy, Billy," I told him. "Keep your faith and trust in me. Together we can do this if you just believe."

"I do believe," he said.

"All right," I whispered, wrapping my arms around him. Then, away from his father, I elevated us into a veil of red mist. Willing my powers to heal the child, I saw visions of the accident flash before my eyes. I could see him running down a burning staircase, see the heavy beam falling onto his foot. Imagining my powers lifting the beam, I felt his suffering pass through my body. Like a sunrise of energy, the red mist began to change color, from orange to yellow to a glowing bright light. It was as if the child's innocence was creating an angelic light as my powers continued to heal his body. Soon it was over. Billy was free, and as I carried him down to run to his father, I too felt free. Disappearing out of sight, I watched from a distance, a father and son unite as one. The sound of laughter, the sound of hope, the sound of life, and so my time in Padstowe was over.

A WALK IN THE SUN

CHAPTER ELEVEN

MY RETURN TO PARIS

They say that one can never go back.
That time is a healer, a sun destined to rise.
Last night I returned to Paris
To a city of love that was no more
Familiar places I knew so well, whispered in sorrow
through the weeping black rain.
A promise of tomorrow had turned to dust.
My Elena had died, and so had my world.

I remembered a moment when I thought nothing could change, that as sure as the autumn leaves would turn golden brown the seasons of Elena's and my love would last forever. Last night I found myself lost in my grief. I was back at the house, and she was gone. Exhausted and confused, I cried for the night to disappear, but as the sun lifted and I escaped to my room, the pain of being alone hit me harder than ever before. Elena was dead. Her bed was empty. I couldn't hear her voice. I couldn't see her smile. I couldn't hold her. I couldn't kiss her, and God knows I just couldn't submit to the fact that she was gone. If I'd told her I loved her a thousand times or more, it could never have been enough, not now, not ever. Death was a cruel game that entangled our emotions, leaving us vulnerable, questioning our actions. Had I truly shown her that she was my world? Could I have done more to express my devotion to her?

When she'd asked me to make her a vampire, I didn't because I loved her. I was sure she'd accepted that I was right, but now I feared I'd ignored the one thing that mattered most to her. Being a vampire would have saved her life, but I'd chosen against it, not wanting her to suffer my immortal curse. Would I have made the same decision if I were given a second chance? I didn't know any more, and it was all too late. No whys or ifs were ever going to bring her back to me.

"I swear to you, Elena," I spoke out to her. "I will never give up until Du Fay pays for what he did to you. I will never give up until he's dead."

As I thought about killing him, I was forced to face the facts. I needed the next few days to regain my strength. My journey from Padstow had proved long and rough. Surviving on rats was hardly enough to feed the life-force of a vampire. I realized now that killing Du Fay was going to take more than just a vampire's physical strength. My instincts had to be sharp, my mind unbreakable. Du Fay knew my weaknesses. He knew my pain, and while my grieving wounds were still bleeding, he could taste the victory upon his blood-drenched hands. For a while I lay, just trying to rest until finally my body surrendered and like an anchor at sea, I sank into a deep, black sleep.

It didn't seem long before I awoke to find I had slept like a worn-out child. Desperately hungry, I needed blood. Tonight Paris would become my feeding ground. Vanishing to the streets, I began my hunt. From the bright lights of the Champs Elysees to the free-spirited streets of St. Germaine, I scanned the night like a ravenous wolf. Along the boulevards, past the bistros and bustling crowds, I started to sense my next victim.

While dancers and poets colored the night, my instincts were leading me toward my purpose. Suddenly I felt him brush my shoulder, a cold-blooded murderer rushing through the square. I could see what he'd done. I could read his mind. His crime was arousing his energy. It was fueling his thoughts.

He had murdered a young girl only a few blocks away, leaving her half-naked corpse in an overgrown churchyard. Her body had been stabbed numerous times, her undergarments torn off, her face badly beaten.

Smelling the stale perfume lingering from his jacket, I could see the blood beneath his tobacco-stained fingernails. Lifting his collar, he hid the scratches on his neck. The last girl he'd killed hadn't fought back like this one. Escaping the nightlife, he slipped down a side street. Then taking a short cut, he sealed his fate.

Down an empty alleyway, he thought he was safe, but I was ready to kill. The blood of a psychopath was at my mercy. Into the air I leaped, then swept down on my target, and in a fury of hunger, I ripped out his throat. Blood and more blood, I drank and drank, absorbing the power that fired everything inside of me. Fleeing the alleyway, I headed back to the square. All I needed was another two days, two days to rest, two more nights of blood. I had to be prepared mentally and physically to be able to overcome anything Du Fay might summon to try to kill me.

Already I began to sense Du Fay's web of destruction weaving in and out of my troubled mind. I knew he had returned to Versailles. I was certain of it. I could feel him watching me. I could feel him challenging my every emotion. Du Fay was pushing me to make a mistake. He knew I needed more time to regain my strength, but he was a coward. His battles weren't won, they were stolen. Just like the devil, Du Fay's triumphs were empty. He would do anything to make me rush to Versailles, anything to create an easy victory for himself. In Cornwall I had witnessed the depraved works of a black magician. Du Fay's powers were immense, his mind-force dangerously brilliant. But still, he was nothing but a psychopathic killer who'd been given the devil's tools to play with.

As I tried not to allow him to invade my thoughts, a vision of Elena flashed before me. Then all at once I saw her tortured body covered in blood. I saw the silver poker protruding out of her chest. Shaking with fury, I begged my powers to give me strength. I knew what Du Fay was trying to do. He was willing me to fight him that very night. Through my own silent screams, Du Fay's whispers became louder, challenging me to fight, calling me a coward. Louder and louder, his voice turned to rage. Then suddenly it stopped, and I collapsed disorientated onto the chapel steps.

My heart was racing as I thought about Elena. My stomach was twisting as I thought about her pain. Du Fay was playing me like a game of chess, setting a trap to cause my own demise. Needing, wanting, waiting to kill him, I told myself to hold back and not be a fool. As much as I wanted to rush to Versailles, I wasn't ready, I needed more time. I was mentally exhausted, mentally derailed. The fact that I hadn't been able to kill Du Fay had taken its toll in more ways than one. Anger and frustration, a vampire's revenge. In Cornwall, Du Fay had thrown me off track. "Never again," I promised myself. "Never again."

As the force of his darkness began to disappear, I pulled myself up and inhaled the night air. Carolers began to sing at the steps of the chapel, reminding me that Christmas was a few weeks away. The smell of roasted chestnuts took me back to my childhood, back to when Charlotte, my nanny, would roast them for me. I remembered every Christmas she would always knit me a scarf and sit with me in the kitchen so I could watch her bake my favorite pie. There were never festive celebrations that included my father, but at least with Charlotte I knew I was loved. How I wished I could have thanked her for her kindness. How I wished I could have held both Charlotte and Elena in my arms.

They had loved me without judgment or doubt. One like a mother; the other like an angel. Two women, two hearts, two faces I adored. Each of them a memory forever alive in my heart.

Continuing to wander alone with my memories, I thought about Francis, the wise old man I had given the emeralds to. I thought about how he had welcomed me into his home the night before he left for Cornwall. He had warned me about Du Fay's dealings in black magic, and had asked me to visit him on my return.

With nowhere else to go, I decided to call on him. Across the street from his home, I stopped for a moment noticing the painted sign above Francis' shop, "Le Petit Violin," a simple name, a simple honesty that reflected the old man's heart and soul. I watched his silhouette playing his violin by the window. As the shadow of his spirit warmed the cold empty street, the faint sound of his violin softened the winter breeze. My friend was home, and for a few minutes I just stood and listened.

The unfamiliar melody was hauntingly beautiful. Its melancholy wistfulness awakened one's soul. Francis was a musician who lived and breathed for his art. His gift was rare. He was so much more than just a talented violinist. His passion when playing expressed a moment, the kind of moment we all wished we could experience. I was proud to have helped him, glad to be able to share his company.

I hoped he wouldn't mind me visiting him at night, and as it turned out, he didn't. He was pleased to see me.

Inviting me in, he welcomed me like an old friend. "I've been worried about you," he said insisting I sit by the fire to get warm. "I prayed you'd be safe whilst you were away." Appreciating his genuine concern, I thanked him for the wine as he sat and joined me.

"You look tired my friend. Traveling this time of year across the harsh sea is no easy journey. When did you get back?"

"Yesterday," I answered. "But the hardest part of my journey was returning to the house, knowing Elena wasn't there. I know it sounds crazy Francis, but I just can't accept I'll never see her again."

He leaned forward and touched my hand. "It doesn't sound crazy, Nicholas. Everything you are feeling is absolutely normal. It is going to take time, a lot of time before you are able to heal and come to terms with her death." He looked at me with tearful eyes, surely knowing the pain and anger I was feeling. He knew Elena's life had ended way too soon. "When I lost my wife, I thought I'd never find the strength to go on, but we do." He sighed tearfully. "Believe me, Nicholas, we do."

Sitting back, he allowed me to think without making me feel I had to answer. Francis was easy company. He had a calmness about him, a restful way that didn't force conversation.

As he stood to add some logs on the fire, I said, "Your suspicions about Du Fay were correct. Everything you told me about him practicing black magic is true."

Frances sat down, his expression worried. "Did you see him in Cornwall?"

"Yes, I saw him, but I didn't get to kill him. I could have, but I didn't."

"Do you want to tell me what happened ? You can trust me. I promise nothing you say will go further than this room."

"I know that," I said, eager to share what I'd discovered in Cornwall. "When I found Du Fay, I discovered the sacrilegious truth of his underworld of evil. He wasn't alone. He has followers, a group of disciples. All of them devil worshippers. The night I broke into Du Fay's house in Wadebridge, he and his disciples had planned to sacrifice an innocent child. At first I didn't see the boy. He was covered with a cloth upon the altar. I hid and watched from the back of their Satanic Temple, waiting for the right moment to kill Du Fay. As he began to summons something hideous above the altar, I tried to get to him, but one of his servants spotted me in the shadows. At that second, all hell broke loose. I was fighting them all, trying to stop Du Fay from escaping. It wasn't until he attacked me with a dagger that I managed to stab him in the arm. If I hadn't had heard the child scream out behind me, I would have finished him. He wouldn't have gotten away."

"What about the child?" Francis asked. "What happened to the boy?"

"I saved him," I answered. "It was horrible. The beast Du Fay had summoned was about to attack the boy. I can still picture it panting madly over the child's naked body. Looking back, I don't know how I managed to get us both out alive, but I did, and as far as I know, the boy's going to be all right. The next day I went back to find Du Fay, but he'd already gone, leaving not a trace of evidence behind him."

"What a monster." Francis shook his head. "The man's a monster." "It makes me think back," he said, "to that morning in the square when they found the missing girl's brother with his head severed on the church steps. It was as if the devil were standing amongst us, waiting and watching to strike again. All those girls he's murdered, and now Elena." He paused as his eyes swelled with tears. "Forgive me, I didn't mean to mention Elena, but hearing about the child and what Du Fay planned to do....."

"It's all right," I assured him. "Next time Du Fay won't escape."

Seeing my frustration, Francis tried to console me. "Don't worry your time will come again. Du Fay cannot hide forever."

"He's not hiding," I answered. "He's back in Versailles."

"How do you know this ?"

"Because my instincts tell me so, and in two days, I intend to go there. Our fight will end in Versailles. I will kill him within the walls he believes to be his fortress of protection."

Francis listened, absorbing my every word. "Maybe I should go with you. There must be something I can do to help you."

Moved by the old man's endearing support, I answered in a way that didn't offend him. "Francis, you have already helped me. Just being here, being able to talk to you and trust you like this. You are my friend. I will not and cannot put you in harm's way. Du Fay knows nothing about you. Let's keep it that way. I've seen how Du Fay works. His powers are great, but that does not change that he's the devil's coward. He thinks he can defeat me, but he is wrong. I am the worst kind of enemy Du Fay could have. When he murdered Elena, he murdered my world. I am the enemy with nothing to lose and nothing to live for. I am willing to die to see justice done."

I felt like telling Francis that I was a vampire, but I didn't. I held back. It was too soon, too disturbing to go into detail. As much as I trusted the old man, I didn't want to scare him. I needed his friendship, not his fear. Trying to convince him not to worry, I rested my hand on his shoulder, allowing him to read the determination in my eyes. "Du Fay realizes that I am no easy target. He has witnessed my strength. He knows what I am. There are things about me I have yet to tell you. Powers I have been given for reasons even I do not understand. Trust me, when this war is over. I will explain everything, but now is not the time."

He stared back at me with a deep sense of understanding. " You don't have to explain anything to me. Your gift is something I would never question. Your heart and courage has already expressed who you are. I feel blessed to know you, blessed to have you in my life."

Touched by his warm words, I thanked him as he poured us some more wine. Sitting back down, he gave a settling smile. "I have something I want to show you." Taking a silver pocket watch from his tatty grey cardigan, he placed it in front of me. I looked down at the time-worn watch and noticed a loose emerald beneath its face. "I saved one of the jewels you gave me. I keep it in here for safety. I like to think of it as my lucky charm."

Remembering the handful of pebbles I had changed into emeralds, I brushed my fingers over its face. Francis sat forward. "I want to leave this watch to you if anything should happen to me, Nicholas. It belonged to my grandfather on my mother's side. Though the watch itself is not worth a lot of money, the soul of its memories is priceless."

Touched by his affection, I asked, "Are you sure?"

"I have never been more certain," he said. "Your kindness adds to the memories of this watch. Your name has already engraved itself in its soul."

As he placed it back in his pocket, I thought about my grandparents who had passed away before I was born. For a few dreamlike seconds, I felt I was a boy again, and Francis was the grandfather I had always wished for. Though I had only known him a short time, there was something about him that made me feel accepted and self-assured. Something my father had never allowed me to feel. Again I felt I wanted to tell him about my life and how a whirlwind of fate had made me become a vampire. In time, I thought, but not now.

As I glanced across the room, I noticed Francis' violin by the window, and thought about the unfamiliar piece I'd heard him playing earlier. I wondered what had inspired him to become a musician and mentioned how much I'd enjoyed listening to him play while I'd waited outside.

His eyes softened, appreciating my comment. Resting in front of the fire, he sighed reflectively and held out his time-honored hands. "These old fingers are not as supple as they used to be, but I thank God every day that they can still play. Age is a funny thing, Nicholas. With it comes experience and understanding, challenged with a child-like frustration that reminds us that we are not as young as our hearts would like us to believe. Silly, everyday duties become an effort." He chuckled. "Like climbing out of bed or bending down to tie one's shoes. Thank goodness I have my music. It's the only thing that reminds me I'm still useful. What about you, Nicholas? Do you play an instrument?"

"No," I answered. "My father didn't encourage music in the house. Unfortunately, learning an instrument wasn't an option."

"I see." Francis nodded. "I remember my father wasn't enthusiastic about my learning to play the violin. It was my mother who encouraged me. She would say a life without music was like a garden without flowers. A simple thought, but how right she was."

"Did your mother play the violin?" I asked.

"No, but her ear for music and tone was remarkable. She had a talent for being able to pick out a good melody. Many times I look back and wish she could have had the opportunities she deserved. But being married to my father meant tolerating a life of hardship. She had to work long hours to keep a roof over our head."

"And your father? What did he do?"

"He was a coach driver. My father spent most of his time away and, whenever he did decide to return home, he spent his earnings either gambling or drinking."

"So who taught you to master the violin?"

Reminiscing, Francis smiled, "It is a long story. Are you sure you want me to go on?"

"Yes," I insisted.

Placing his wine back on the table, he sat back. "My mother worked long hours. Well she cleaned for a very well- respected family across town, the Grey family. They had a beautiful home, a big house. The kind of house a child dreams of playing in. So many rooms and stairs, so many trees to climb inside their grounds. Most afternoons I would wait for my mother outside the gates and then one day Mr. Potts, the butler, began allowing me to wait for my mother in the kitchens. He was a nice man, strict but kind. I think he understood my mother's situation more than he let on. It was there whilst I would have a glass of milk and a piece of leftover cake that I began to hear stories about Mr. Grey, the master of the house. He was a professor of music, a highly respected violinist whose pupils came from near and far to have him teach them. Every Friday afternoon he would return home and shut the doors of his sitting room to play and compose. No one, not even Mrs. Grey or his two children, were allowed to disturb him. Unbeknown to my mother or the other servants, I would sometimes sneak out of the kitchen and make my way around the side of the house where I could listen to him play. It was there, hidden amongst the bushes beneath the open window of the sitting room, that my passion for music really began. I had never heard anything so moving and magical. The way he played. The God-given melodies I'd hear him put together. Every note. Every pause. Every cry of his instrument painted a picture that breathed with emotion. I was a ten-year-old boy dreaming beneath that window of a world outside the one I lived in. For weeks every Friday I sneaked out to the same spot. But one afternoon, when I was feeling adventurous and decided to stand and watch him play, I was caught by his daughter Emily

I remember Master Grey listening to his daughter exaggerating how she found me. He didn't appear angry. In fact he hushed her down and asked her to leave so he could speak to me alone. When I mentioned my mother cleaned for him and unbeknown to her, I'd been hiding in the bushes to listen to him, he smiled forgivingly. Looking amused, he told me that neither one of his children showed any enthusiasm for his work. In fact, both were adamant they didn't want to learn the violin. I remember being puzzled and asking why, but he didn't answer me. Instead he pondered and stared thoughtfully as if he could read how desperately I wanted to learn. Before I left, he invited me to join him the following Friday, and when I did, I realized he'd made a decision that would change my life forever. Master Grey became my teacher, and for the next three and a half years, every Friday afternoon, he taught me as if I were a part of his family. I was allowed to borrow a violin to practice at home. I was allowed to have sandwiches in the sitting room after my lesson. It was unbelievable, a dream come true for a poor boy who had nothing more to offer than his willingness to learn.

Listening to my wise friend made me realize how much I had to learn. Pulling himself up from his seat, he walked over to what appeared to be an old storage bench.

Removing the seat cushions, he lifted the lid and reached down, taking out a worn violin case. "This is where I keep my faithful old friend." Carefully, he carried it across the room and sat it down in front of me. "I was lucky to have found her again after she had been taken away from me, but thanks to the angels it wasn't long before I discovered her in the window of a local pawn shop."

"You had it taken?"

"Yes, the night you found me homeless, I'd had most of my belongings taken from me. With your help Nicholas, I was able to buy her back." Using his sleeve, he brushed the dust from the top of its case and snapped open the discolored clasps. "This is the violin Master Grey gave to me," he said, taking it out of the case.

"Do you still play it?" I asked.

"No, not now." His eyes softened as his fingers gently stroked the strings. "There was a time our love affair was unstoppable, but the years have taken their toll." Pausing for a minute, he held it in his hands as if he were listening to the music of their past. "You know," he sighed tenderly, "some things are not meant to be restored, just treasured." He gently placed it back in its case. "When I am gone, this too will be yours, but until then, I shall look after her."

As we finished our wine, a trusting silence seemed to bind the pages of our fated friendship. Though our conversation had left me thinking about my father, I never mentioned him. I couldn't risk the anchor of my childhood dragging me down into a sea of insecurity. I wasn't that frail boy crying in the dark anymore. I was a man, a vampire who was no longer afraid.

Francis sat quietly respecting my silence. His experiences of life and its challenges had given him the gift of wisdom and insight. Most would have described the deep lines on his face as just plain old age, but to me, they expressed a composition of his life and spirit.

That night when I left, he hugged me like a concerned father. "You don't have to leave, Nicholas," he said. "My home is your home."

Thanking him again, I continued to make my way downstairs.

"Will I see you tomorrow?" he asked.

Thinking about Du Fay, I answered, "If not tomorrow, in a few days."

"But, Nicholas..." He stopped me nervously.

"Do not worry Francis, I will see you when I return from Versailles."

Away from the comfort of Francis's home, I made my way back to the house to rest until the following night. Beneath the full moon I felt the first kiss of winter touch my cheek as the virgin snow began to fall. Like God's confetti, it sprinkled the darkness laying a blanket of light over the city. I stopped for a moment and welcomed its purity, remembering a time when I could watch the season's change. How I missed the beauty of the morning sun—the birds, the blue sky, the warmth of a new day.

I had never had the chance to share that with Elena, and she had never complained, not once, not ever. Memories of what could have been passed before my eyes. I thought about Elena, my father, and Charlotte, all of them gone too soon. Was it the wind or my grieving imagination hearing my father's whispers echoing through the branches of the snow-covered trees? It was as if his spirit was here beside me, asking for forgiveness, telling me to be strong. For what it was worth, I held on to that feeling. For what harm would it do to believe the wind?

Chapter Twelve

A Battle for Justice

I am a broken branch
Lying beneath the tree of justice.
I pray that one day my naked arms
Might feel the spring leaves of a new tomorrow.

Last night, I listened to the voice of winter. The ghostlike messages I imagined to be my father's had now gone away as I awoke in silence. For the first time since leaving Cornwall, I felt my powers had returned. I was ready to fight the devil and Du Fay, ready to face his world of evil. Without God on my side, I stood alone. But even a vampire had the right to believe. As crazy as it seemed, I was taking Charlotte's gift to me, the cross and chain. That cross would serve as my shield of faith. The last time I'd touched it, it had ignited in my hand, but the fire of God's fury hadn't made me renounce the power of its meaning. This time I knew not to open the box. I just placed it in my pocket and left the house.

Outside, my carriage waited. The snow had melted making it easier to reach Versailles within a couple of hours. Was it my suspicious mood, or did the air feel hauntingly heavy and calm? It was as if the night recognized my fury simmering beneath the depth of my grief. Du Fay was expecting me. I sensed his revenge. He'd been waiting for this night to prove his supremacy. He needed to kill me but more important, he needed to affirm his position of power. My mission was less complicated and written in stone. Du Fay was going to die, and nothing else mattered. Determined and eager, I asked my driver to hurry to Versailles, but as soon as we turned the corner, I began to sense something was wrong. Du Fay's presence hovered inside the carriage, a ghost-like presence that seemed to breathe in my ear.

"Your powers have failed you, Justine," his demonic voice whispered in my head. "Again you were careless, and again you lose. You should never have left the old man alone."

As the echoes of his madness laughed cruelly in my head, visions of Francis flashed before my eyes. He was lying in a hospital bed grasping for breath, his bloody face and hands, blackened from the smoke of a fire. Stopping the coach, I ran outside. He needed my help. I had to fly. Du Fay had been to Francis' home and had set fire to his shop. I could see the flames, the orange-lit sky, violent images that shook my mind.

Away from the street, I shot into the sky, determined not to let Francis die. With fists clenched and my body in line like a human arrow, I bolted against the wind. High above the rooftops across the city, I spotted the fire, the mayhem, the screams as everyone panicked to help put out the flames. Francis was at the hospital. I had to get to him. Struggling not to lose my mind, I tried to stay focused. Anger and frustration would only work against me. If Francis were still alive, I had to remain calm. I couldn't let my fury get in the way of my purpose. To heal him, he would have to believe in me, believe in himself, his light that connected his body and soul. If he was unconscious, I might not be able to do anything. Oh God. As I raced to save him, I blamed myself. I should have known this could happen. I should never have gone to Francis' home. I should never have put his life in danger. The devil had outplayed me, and I'd allowed it to happen.

For all my hope of finding Francis alive when I reached the hospital, I was forced to face the unbearable truth. My friend had passed away moments before I had arrived. I was too late. In a daze of helplessness, I listened to the doctor explain how Francis had tried to hold on. He also told me that he was convinced my friend had been a victim of a brutal attack.

"There were vicious wounds," he said, "cuts and bruises that were clearly unrelated to the fire. We did everything we could, but the damage to his lungs caused by the smoke was too much for a man of his age."

Feeling my blood boil with rage, I wanted to tear Du Fay apart limb by limb. "Soon," I told myself fighting my fury. I had just lost my friend. I needed to see him one last time. After asking the doctor to allow me a few minutes alone with him, I walked in the room and closed the door as if he were sleeping. Last night I had seen the life in my friend's eyes, recognized the wisdom in each line of his face. Tonight his story was unrecognizable. The cuts, the bruises, the burns were too much to bear, too painful to look at.

His cardigan had been thrown in the corner. I picked it up and felt something in the pocket. It was his watch, his treasured possession, a lifetime of his memories resting in my hand. He had wanted me to take care of it, like a trusting son.

Overcome with emotion, I stared at the loose emerald beneath its face and remembered his words from last night. "I like to think of it as my good luck charm," he'd said. His voice still echoed in my heart.

"If only," I said. " If only that had been true." I took the stone out of its face, placed it in his hand and gently closed his fingers around it. "This belongs with you, my friend," I whispered. "I should have told you I was a vampire. I am so sorry Francis. I am so sorry for bringing you into my world."

Still holding his watch, I dipped my head, asking his soul to forgive my ignorance. Then I moved away from his bedside, swallowed my tears, and said, "Goodbye."

From sorrow, to silent rage, to facing reality, I went through the motions of all the necessary paperwork. Francis' body would be brought to my house after the coroner had finished his report.

Out on the street, I raced to kill, unleashing the fury of my own errors. Another torturous lesson, another nightmare of regret. Another innocent life taken, another message from a madman. Du Fay had caught me off guard. He had played me like a puppet hanging from a string. I'd allowed myself to weaken, needing the comfort of a friend. My own self pity had put Francis in danger, and now it was too late. Francis was dead.

"Damn you, Du Fay! Damn you to hell," I shouted. "You are going to die. This time you will not live to see another sunrise."

Not wanting to waste an ounce of my strength by flying, I hurried into a waiting carriage and sped away toward Versailles. Leaning out the window, I banged on the roof. "Faster man, faster. " Away from the city, we raced through the countryside until I recognized the opening in the woods. "Slow down," I yelled, spotting the obscure turning. "Stop." I leapt from of the carriage. Then I gave the driver a handful of money and said, "Leave."

"But sir, these woods aren't safe at night. The town is still a way ahead."

"I insist, now leave," I ordered, frantic to move ahead.

"As you wish," he said, pushing the money into his pocket.

I watched the coach vanish into the distance and took to the air beneath the watching sky. There wasn't much time, only two hours before sunrise.

Flying through the moonlit forest, I caught sight of Du Fay's house of death. This time fire torches lit the walls and gates. He was waiting, watching, and enjoying my fury.

As I descended beyond the towering gates, my mind flashed back to Elena's tortured body. This time, this night was all I lived for. My battle for justice was about to begin. Getting ready to smash my way inside, I saw the black doors open wide. Like the devil's mouth, it breathed out its evil, hungry to devour its next victim. Undaunted by the invisible force, I crossed the threshold into the arena of Du Fay's sordid world. All at once I heard the doors bang shut behind me, followed by the slam of heavy bolts locking themselves firmly in place. It was a pathetic display of cowardly magic that would have caused any mortal to tremble with fear.

I was a vampire. Locks and bolts were of no consequence to me. Du Fay's useless tricks were irrelevant and meaningless, a sick display of a coward at work. Shifting forward, I could taste his presence, smell his blood like an open wound. Across the hall I noticed another door open, then all at once I heard Du Fay call out like thunder,

"I've been expecting you, Justine. It is time you came to face your Master!"

I charged toward him, but his powers threw me back.

"Another mistake." He smiled sadistically. "Did you really believe it would be that easy?" Standing by the hearth inside his library, his onyx eyes beamed with conviction. "You are out of your depth, vampire. To presume you could come here and enter my house, my domain and try to defeat me makes you an even bigger fool than I perceived you to be. You cannot come near me unless I allow it. The shield of my will protects this room. It can protect any place in this house I forbid you to enter. Do you understand? Or does my profound power confuse you?"

Unafraid of his dominance, I attempted to get through the doorway, but again I was forced back, unable to get through his invisible wall. Du Fay looked on, displaying his contempt, lighting a cigar with a mocking expression.

"Your attempts are tiresome, to say the least, boring and unschooled. I almost feel sorry for you. Haven't you realized your limitations yet?"

Watching him in front of me, and not being able to kill him, was unbearable. "You say you are so powerful, and yet you hide like a coward, too scared to fight. What's wrong Du Fay? Aren't you strong enough to destroy me, or can you only slaughter the helpless and weak? Do you believe killing, sacrificing women and children makes you powerful and supreme? Tonight you killed another defenseless victim who couldn't fight back. You are nothing, Du Fay. Nothing but a gutless murderer sheltered by the devil!"

"How admirable." His eyes blazed with anger and sarcasm. "A vampire with a conscience. Should I praise you or pity you before I kill you?"

"Mock all you want, but tonight you are the one who will die," I said. "This house will crumble with you and its demons buried beneath it. Don't threaten me behind your wall of fear. Come out and fight."

Suddenly Du Fay's mouth stiffened. His mask of unconcern disappeared. "Be careful," he growled. "Courage without knowledge is a dangerous pastime. You threaten like a schoolboy standing in a playground. Believe me, Vampire, this isn't a playground. There are no safety nets or second chances to be had inside these walls. Your nocturnal powers are useless here. Tonight you will die, but not before you are taught a lesson."

"What lesson?" I retorted. "Is this the result of a great magician? No, this hell you created only demonstrates that you're a deranged monster who sold his soul to the devil. When you murdered Elena, you sealed your fate. You became the hunted, and you sentenced yourself to death."

He began walking toward me, and I could see his demons crawling inside his heartless body. Spitting out his rage, he said, "I am tired of your rambling threats. You and your kind sicken me. Do you think you are the first vampire I have had to suffer? Do you think I don't know how you creatures work? I have killed stronger and greater vampires than you, Justine. Vampires that have survived for centuries, whose insight and powers are beyond your grasp. You are dull, a simple-minded waste of my time, a pathetic result of your nocturnal breed. Is it any wonder why your father damned the day you were born? It must have been difficult being cast aside like some stray dog that didn't belong."

"You know nothing about my life or my father," I told him, feeling myself break into a sweat. "Our relationship was something you could never understand!"

"Relationship?" Du Fay laughed. "What relationship? He despised you until the day he died."

"I know what you are trying to do," I replied, "and it won't work. You never knew my father, and even if you had, I am certain he never would have befriended you."

"I never said we were friends," Du Fay replied coolly. "I said we had met. Your father came to Paris often. The first time we were introduced, I distinctly remember him telling me he had no children. You can't cover up the truth, and fantasizing about your father doesn't make it real. The fact that you choose to wear his ring only shows how desperate you truly are."

"My father was not my world." I kept my voice even and strong. "Elena was my world, and you will pay for what you did to her."

Du Fay glared with satisfaction. "And what exactly do you intend to do to me, Justine? You are fighting a losing battle. If you had wanted to keep her, you should have made her a vampire instead of leaving her alone day after day. It was only a matter of time before another one of your fantasies would be shattered. Would you leave a diamond necklace out on the street and expect no one to take it?"

Trembling with fury, I tried again to smash through Du Fay's invisible wall.

"You see," he said with a smirk, "the time has come for you to face the truth. No more excuses, no more lying to yourself. You chose to leave Elena unprotected. Vampires like you aren't powerful enough to protect a mortal, let alone yourself when the sun begins to rise. How do I know this? Because I am the master of the sacred underworld. I am the master who sees and understands the powers of the universe. I gave Elena a choice. She could have been a part of my world. I offered her more than any vampire could have given her, but unfortunately, her ignorance sealed her own fate."

"Fate?" I asked. "Slaughtering her in cold blood, making her suffer, ending her life, you call that fate? Your diseased mind belongs in an asylum. You killed Elena because you couldn't change her heart. Tonight, you shield yourself because you are too scared to fight, too scared to die. You can only slaughter the weak, the vulnerable, the helpless."

Du Fay's eyes charged with fury. He did not answer, but a bluish glow began to radiate from his body. Then all at once he raised his outstretched hand. Staring directly into his palm, I watched the veins in his forehead begin to swell. His face became fixed in deep concentration as he began to whisper strange words beneath his breath.

Marking his every move, I knew that, at any moment, some new horror could appear to join him. His wall of protection still stood between us, but Du Fay had a plan, and I could feel his energy growing stronger.

Just then, a flash of light burst out from his palm, and all at once, by magic, he drew out a silver dagger. Grasping his weapon, he pointed it toward me like some great magician commanding the stage. With glazed black eyes, he called out, "I demand the gates of my unyielding will to be removed from the threshold of this room."

I felt the floor begin to tremble, and I was thrown back with the force of his iron command. Du Fay didn't move. He just watched and waited, his expression unaltered, his eyes like stone.

"It is time, Justine," he said as if he were invincible. "The game is over."

With all my might, I flew toward him, refusing to believe his powers could beat me. Du Fay leapt back, slashing his dagger, commanding the furniture to block my attack. Trying to grab him, I spotted the crossed swords above the doorway as Du Fay called out ordering them to kill me. This time his magic had sealed his own fate. Shooting through the air, I caught both swords and instantly drove them through his chest.

It was then I realized I had been tricked all along. The swords and my body had flown through an illusion, an illusion I had believed to be Du Fay. Turning around in a maze of horror, I could see the ghost-like vision slowly fading. I gazed in shock and disbelief. How was it possible? How had he done it? Du Fay had spoken to me. He had answered me, attacked me. He had been in this room. I wasn't wrong, but how was I right? Du Fay wasn't here.

Thrown into a web of confusion and doubt, I felt trapped inside Du Fay's wicked game. I should never have chosen to fight him here. He had planned his every move, and I was losing. How could I defeat an illusion, a specter? I tried telling myself not to weaken. Du Fay was not invincible. It was in that moment of uncertainty, that moment of question, when I felt something plunge into my back. Before I could turn around, I was stabbed again. This time the knife had struck my heart. Feeling an explosion of agonizing pain, I collapsed on the floor, unable to move.

"Look at me, Vampire," Du Fay spat. "Have your powers forsaken you? Is this the best you can do? "

Gasping for breath, I knew I was dying. My wound had not healed. I had no strength. Kicking me in the face, Du Fay watched me bleed, enjoying his victory as I lay helpless before him.

"Lesson number one," he said. "Never use the eyes to seek out your enemy. I warned you, Justine. Ignorance is not bliss in my world."

As he growled his words, suddenly he was thrown across the room. Then all at once, I heard a voice roar like thunder. "And ignorance is not bliss in my world, Du Fay! Did you really believe you could kill my son? "

Staring through a blur of dying vision, I thought I saw my father standing in the doorway—his beaming red eyes, his chalk-white face, his mouth stretched back bearing the fangs of a vampire. It couldn't be. I gasped, struggling to remain conscious. My father a vampire? My father was dead!

"I thought I killed you," Du Fay said, without fear. "I was sure you were dead."

"Never presume a victory against a vampire, Du Fay. Especially one with the power to destroy you. "

Recognizing my father's voice, I knew I wasn't hallucinating. Like a weapon of destruction, he shot threw the air and hurled Du Fay across the room. Crashing against the library wall, Du Fay dropped to the floor striking his head. The last I remembered, Du Fay was running toward the door, bleeding, panicking, trying to escape. Almost unconscious, I felt someone shaking me, forcing me to wake up, calling out my name. Then through my disoriented haze, I saw my father. He shook me again, grasping my shoulders.

"Nicholas, Nicholas, you must wake up," he said. "We haven't much time. I need you to listen to me. Your wound is deep, but you are not going to die. I am going to help you, but you have to believe in your immortal powers. Do you hear me, Nicholas? You cannot and must not doubt the powers you have been given."

Then he cut his wrist, and his eyes filled with emotion. "Drink, my son. Your wound will heal. My blood is your blood. Together we are strong."

Desperate to stay alive, I drank my father's blood as he continued to speak to me. "I know why you came here, Nicholas. Du Fay is still alive, but soon you will have your justice."

Feeling my body gaining strength, I closed my eyes and began to see images of my father's past. Visions of his life flashed before me, visions that didn't stop when I opened my eyes. It was as if I had become trapped inside my father's emotions. Four hundred years of blood and decay. Four hundred years he continued to live. A vampire's survival, a vampire's war. I could see his past, his fury, his despair. Century after century, his world unfolded. Books he had written, music he had composed, undeniable gifts of a vampire's heart. A brilliant solicitor, respected and honored, a profession that became his ultimate cover. Out of the darkness and into the light, in an instant, I was looking at a portrait of my mother. I recognized the painting in my father's study, my father's work, the anonymous artist. A thousand chapters, a thousand tears, an immortal gallery of passion and pain. He had found his sunrise in my mother's eyes. And within that sunrise, I realized he had always loved me.

Now, the visions began to fade. I was back in the library staring back at my father. If there had ever been a time I had wanted to comfort him, it was then. He spoke in a soft becalming tone, but he couldn't hide the tears in his eyes.

"Your wounds have healed," he said, taking my hand. "Your powers will not weaken. They will only become stronger."

Seeing my father overcome with emotion, I couldn't recall a time he had ever held my hand. It was as if the chains of my childhood had just been broken.

"Nicholas," he said. "I know I cannot change the past, but there is so much I need to tell you, so much you need to know. Since you came to Paris, I have watched you from afar. I have witnessed your courage. I felt your pain. So many times, I've wanted to help you, tried to explain why I chose to disappear. You must believe me, Nicholas. You need to know I have never loved anyone more than you and your mother."

With that, he hugged me. Then, without warning, he shot back out from my arms. Seeing my father thrown through the air, I couldn't stop Du Fay's unexpected attack. I saw the blood, I saw the sword, and I saw the blade protruding from my father's chest. Crying out in horror, I leapt to help him, but at that moment I discovered I wasn't strong enough to overcome Du Fay's might and domination. With one blow, he had thrown me across the room, and with one command, his powers were forcing me back.

"You pathetic fool," he said. "Did you really believe your father could save you? No vampire is immortal. Look at him now, and face the truth. Neither one of you has the power to dethrone my rule. I alone control this underworld of evil. The Prince of Darkness protects my world." Like a deranged dictator, Du Fay carried on, as I watched my world tumbling down once more. My father was dying, and I couldn't break free. My wounds had healed, but I didn't have the strength to kill Du Fay. My father had told me my powers would become stronger, and I knew in my heart he was telling the truth.

"Truth?" Du Fay laughed, reading my mind. "Isn't it obvious your father lied to you? He knows you are weak. Only guilt brought him here. Not love, not regret."

At that moment, I could hear my father's voice begin whispering in my head. "Nicholas, you must concentrate. Don't allow Du Fay to invade your mind. You have the power. Use it. Your heart is your weapon. Do not doubt who you truly are."

Infused with my father's blood, infused by his words, a lifetime of emotions became my strength. It was as if every experience I had survived and overcome had become one meaning, one truth. I was the same man who became a vampire. My heart, my reason had never changed direction. I still believed in God, and I still believed in justice. The devil ruled the night, but he didn't rule me. It was in that moment of faith, that moment of knowing, when I realized that my powers were unstoppable.

Du Fay's army of strength couldn't hold me back. His battlefield of demons couldn't stop my purpose. Bursting toward him, I grabbed him by the neck, as his eyes screamed out his last command. All at once, the heavy drapes flung back from the windows, but the devil and the morning sun would not be his savior. Tearing my fangs into Du Fay's neck, I ripped out his throat feeling his bones crack inside my blood-filled mouth.

Du Fay was dead, but there was no relief. I had to save my father, I couldn't let him die. Turning around, I cried out in despair, as I saw his body disintegrating before me. The suns rays were upon him. My father was disappearing, crumbling into dust before my eyes. Unable to stop his body from fading, I begged my powers to bring him back. No books, no truths could have prepared me for that moment. The reality, the nightmare was too much to bear.

Falling beside his ashes, I grasped his cloak. Derailed and broken, I was lost in confusion. I wanted to hold him, to love him, to save him. He had given me his powers, and I had survived. There was no doubt, no question that I was still a vampire. The blood in my veins had never felt more immortal. Could it be that my father had unlocked my darkness? Had the power of his love given me the sun? My battle with Du Fay was finally over, but victory and defeat had never felt so empty. This time justice had raised a double-edged sword, and the blade of its judgment had cut both ways.

Taking my father's wedding ring, I placed it in my pocket and folded his ashes in his cloak. For the first time in my life, time did not matter. There was no one to love, and nothing left to fight for. Through silence and sorrow, I prayed he could hear me, hear my heart telling him how much I loved him. Unlike the visions portrayed in death, there were no angels by my side. No signs of comfort whispered through the sunlit window.

From the Godless walls of Du Fay's dying mansion, I left for London carrying my father's ashes. Everything my father was, and everything he had proven to be, was enshrined in my heart, my soul, my reason. He had given me the daylight to help set me free. He had given me a vision, a foundation of hope. With the heart of a vampire and the tears of a son, I thanked my father for the morning sky.

I am Nicholas Justine. I am a Vampire, and this is my story -- A Walk in the Sun

EPILOGUE

The winds of Change, the Seasons of time,
And the falling leaves forever define
Naked branches that express life's sorrow
For those we have lost and ask why.

I gaze across the Vampire Vineyards and watch the sun set against a red velvet sky. This place, this soil has become a part of my being, my Chateau du Vampire, my home. I realized many years ago that Justine Manor could never be something its soul could never feel. The night my father saved my life was the first time I understood how much he loved me. That memory, that moment was all I wanted to remember, and for that reason alone, I decided to sell Justine Manor. More than a century has passed since I buried my father's ashes to rest beside my mother's grave. The colors of time in an ever-changing world, but my immortal canvas has remained un-faded. I still close my eyes and imagine my Elena standing in the distance calling my name. Her long red hair blows gently in the breeze, her eyes so much greener than the grass in springtime. For a moment, she is with me. For a moment, I care. For a moment, I breathe. Then suddenly, she is gone. What sorrow, what pain? But I cannot let go, for I know that one day I will find her again. Until then, I live in a vampire's world on the path of immortality that forever reflects the footsteps of my past. Change creates wisdom; wisdom creates change, but the truth remains simple if we accept its innocence.

What happened the day I buried my father's ashes was a miracle that had grown from a seed of compassion. Francis, my friend who I thought had died was instead alive and came to find me. The emerald I had left inside his hand had brought about a miracle I never thought possible. The powers of empathy had healed the old man, and we remained dear friends until the day he died a natural death. Now more than a century later, his memory still warms my heart.

These are the memories that helped guide me forward, that helped me accept who I am today. Blood is my life-force. That, I cannot change. But the choices we make define who we are. I hunt to survive, but the innocent remain safe. My victims are those who pray on the helpless.

This is my story, but it's only the beginning, for I know my journey is far from over. Tomorrow and forever, a million sunsets from now, I will find my Elena. I will hold her again. Together we will fly across a vampire sky - two lovers, two hearts, one world immortal. As I watch the sunset against the red velvet sky, I close my journal and await that day.

SPECIAL THANKS.

*T*o my husband Michael for insisting I write this book and to my son Nicholas for cheering me on.

To my parents for their constant love, advice and support.

To all my family and dear friends in England and in Los Angeles. Additional thanks to my editor Bonnie Hearn Hill and designer Don Lewis.

The Vampire Wine Society
visit
Vampire.com

Come Experience a Taste of Immortality

A Midnight Rendezvous at the Vampire Lounge - - -
Los Angeles Times

"The potent wine and other elixirs are attracting nocturnal creatures to the posh den in Beverly Hills. If you're a 500 year old vampire, this is where you'd drink, the Vampire Lounge, a cozy Beverly Hills wine lounge, where the walls are painted buttery gold and the upstairs Vampire Lair has throw pillows on deep velvet couches. With heavy gold mirrors everywhere, it's almost as if it's been designed to taunt your average reflection - dodging light - avoiding Nosferatu."

For VIP Private Parties or Reservations for the Upstairs Vampire Lair,
please call 310 VAMPIRE (826-7473) or
email reservations@vampire.com

ABOUT THE AUTHOR

English writer/musician Lisa Dominique Machat resides in Los Angeles with her husband Michael and 10-year-old son Nicholas. This is Lisa's first novel. Lisa serves as a director of Vampire Vineyards. Lisa and her husband (trademark and music attorney Michael Machat) are the proud owners of Vampire Vineyards. In 2011, Lisa designed and opened the Vampire Lounge & Tasting Room in Beverly Hills.

Preferred Interests – Writing, music, movies and wine.

Favorite Activity -- setting up her deck chair and cheering her son on in his favored passion, soccer.

For more information about Lisa, please visit www.awalkinthesun.com

Made in the USA
Monee, IL
07 October 2022

15408773R00121